paris jungle

I0630782

A NOVEL OF SEXISM
IN THE FINANCE WORLD

ADRIA J. CIMINO

velvet morning
press

Published by Velvet Morning Press

Copyright © 2016, 2018 by Adria J. Cimino

Previously published as *The Creepshow* in 2016

ISBN-13: 978-0-9977676-6-7
ISBN-10: 0-9977676-6-9

Cover design by Ellen Meyer and Vicki Lesage
Author photo by Didier Quémener

Discover more by
BEST-SELLING AUTHOR
ADRIA J. CIMINO

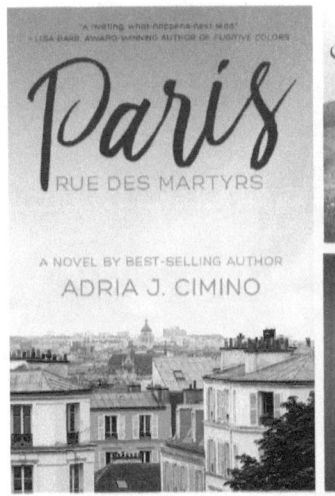

Find out about new releases and deals
by signing up for Adria's newsletter:
https://bit.ly/cimino-news

(She'll even send you *Flore* for free!)

*To those who have looked up and discovered
a glass ceiling overhead*

"Les cons, ça ose tout. C'est même à ça
qu'on les reconnaît."

Michel Audiard, *Les Tontons Flingueurs*,
a film by Georges Lautner, 1963

"Jerks will try anything. That's exactly how
you recognize them."

Prologue

There were two kinds of people at the Creepshow. Those who drank the Kool-Aid and those who pretended to. Both could survive and coexist in the company. Meeting at the water cooler, complaining about how overworked they were and then returning to their desks with self-righteous smiles.

Wanda Julienne belonged to the latter category. At first, she didn't even know it, didn't realize the importance or the implications. She was a young old-timer in the glass tower under-looking the Eiffel Tower. More than a decade earlier, as she was about to graduate from college, a recruiter for Whilt Investment Services Inc. snapped her up for the company's Paris office. Her foreign language and financial skills would make her the perfect addition to the team.

Management immediately liked Wanda's analytic prowess, the way she could run numbers and turn a company's finances inside out, and the way she constructed charts and graphs. But that was simply part of a financial analyst's job, wasn't it? Whilt management quickly promoted her to fund manager and praised her talent for choosing the right investments.

The icing on the cake was that Wanda kept her mouth shut and smiled. Did what she was told, returned to her desk with lowered eyes, didn't count her hours, joined the team at a wine bar after work. She was innocuous.

But with the arrival of interns and fresh faces right out of college, Wanda Julienne was also getting expensive.

As Wanda thought back to the events of that winter two years ago, she asked herself: *Exactly when did everything in my life switch from organized to chaos? Was it the day I started calling Whilt Investment Services "the Creepshow"? Was it when I let my voice be heard? Was it the day my boss reached up my skirt?*

No, it began with the suicide of Elodie Clark.

Chapter 1

For the first time in six months, Wanda Julienne hurried down five flights in high heels. She quickly checked her reflection in the massive mirror hanging in the vestibule of her apartment building. Long brown hair drawn into a smooth ponytail, minimal makeup, stylish trench and overstuffed designer handbag. Other than the fact that her green eyes looked puffy from lack of sleep, and her belly no longer blocked the view of her feet, she looked about the same as the last time she headed out the door for a long day in the office.

But this time, the context was different. She wasn't leaving home with a carefree heart, eagerly thinking about the appointments and tasks ahead. Instead, last-minute questions filled her mind: Would Nelly's fever from the day before come back, and if it did, would the nanny follow her instructions? Would Nelly fuss so much that the nanny would change her mind about watching an infant among her small group of toddlers?

Wanda shook her head as if to rid her mind of the fears and get back to the business at hand. Sure, she had left three-month-old Nelly across the hall at the nanny share for the first time, but this didn't necessarily have to be a bad thing. Wouldn't Nelly, little by little, have a lot more fun with the older children than she would bouncing around in the baby carrier attached to her mother's chest? Of course she would. Wanda pictured the colorful toys scattered in the playroom and the delighted faces of the toddlers when they saw a baby would be joining them. The thought reassured her, and she smiled, feeling a sense of freedom as the cool autumn air caressed her cheeks.

It was time to return to the offices of Whilt Investment Services, and she knew it.

Whilt was an international asset management firm, and Wanda was one of two senior fund managers in the Paris office. She'd left her clients in the hands of Thomas Champlain, a junior fund manager she didn't particularly trust, but Wanda had tried not to think about that as she passed along her files months ago. Her boss, Louis, had appointed Thomas before Wanda even had time to list all of the bad investments Thomas had been responsible for in the past. Now, part of her cringed as she walked the short distance from her apartment to the office.

Then she stopped the destructive chain of thoughts. Perhaps she had underestimated Thomas. Maybe he ended up doing a decent job. Unlikely, but at least the idea comforted her.

A swirl of brittle leaves, buoyed by the wind, rushed before Wanda as if paving the way. She followed, clutching her silk scarf closer to her neck and glancing left and right at the familiar buildings that lined this grand avenue in the ritzy sixteenth arrondissement. The scalloped balconies, stately iron gates and expertly cut hedges painted a picture of elegance.

Along with Wanda's personal and professional worries, feelings of elation also filled her heart. She thought of all that she loved about her job: researching a company's potential, meeting with clients to explain her convictions of why a certain stock was worth their hard-earned money, rushing to after-work drinks with anyone who was able to get out of the office by seven o'clock. Well, the after-work drinks would likely be out of the question for a long while. But everything else would be the same, and that pleased Wanda.

And then, before she could ponder any further, she was standing before the glass doors.

❦

Lunchtime rolled around, and Wanda was still trying to digest the news: Elodie Clark had fallen to her death the night before. Right on the premises. This young mother of two had left a messy leaf angel on the sidewalk below Conference Room A. That was why the meeting room was sealed with duct tape and police officers walked the halls in the morning hours as Wanda settled uncomfortably into her cubicle.

Management said it was an accident, but Wanda didn't buy it. Why would someone lean so far out the window for a breath of fresh air when it was cold and windy outside?

A hand touched her shoulder.

Wanda jumped, then felt her face go hot. She hated being caught when her mind was wandering.

"Join me for lunch." Maddie's calm brown eyes met Wanda's agitated ones. "I know it's difficult to come back, and on a day like today... Well, there couldn't be much worse."

Maddie, about a dozen years older than Wanda, had helped her learn the ropes at Whilt. She now sat in an office upstairs with a position that held fewer and fewer responsibilities as the years progressed. She once told Wanda she didn't care. She had a comfortable inheritance and her husband's large salary to fall back on if her duties ever totaled zero. So far, those duties lingered at a low number, yet high enough to justify her presence.

Maddie didn't spend much time socializing with the "downstairs" crowd—the fund managers and analysts— but always made an exception for Wanda. "For old times' sake," she would say.

Wanda hesitated as she glanced at the stack of mail on her desk and the darkened computer screen. She hadn't been able to log on all morning due to a glitch the techs were still trying to fix. And Thomas had been in out-of-office meetings so couldn't brief her on her funds' performances. In vain, she had approached Louis' office but then turned away when she saw he was embroiled in discussion after discussion with police.

"Clearly, everyone is in shock," Maddie said. "I don't think anyone's going to get much work done today. So how about it?" She tucked her blond bob behind her ears and then crossed her arms across her chest with feigned authoritativeness.

Wanda nodded and grabbed her coat. A silent cloud of shock hung over the office. Hardly a word was said since Wanda had entered the building that morning. Louis' secretary had informed them of the previous night's events and told them to stay at their desks so investigators could do their job.

"Why didn't they close the damn office?" Wanda asked as she and Maddie rounded the corner and made their way a block down to their favorite café.

"And lose a day of productivity, dear?" Maddie snorted and shook her head. "Wanda, you've been out for so long that you've forgotten how Whilt operates? Louis spent an hour early this morning convincing police we were preparing a project for the finance ministry so we couldn't possibly be shut down, even for a day."

"I guess I never saw management deal with suicide."

There. Wanda had said it. The word that had been floating through her mind since she learned of "the accident."

"They'll never say the 's' word," Maddie said, "especially since they know as well as most of us that this place drove Elodie to it. The constant pressure. She had been suffering from depression, her husband lost his job, and here at Whilt, her efforts never seemed to please them." Without missing a beat, Maddie looked up at the approaching waiter. "The usual, times two. Quiche/salad combo still OK, Wanda?"

Wanda nodded, not caring much about the contents of her lunch plate. The Elodie that Wanda remembered was bright and hardworking. Wanda hadn't known her very well since Elodie had been the sort to keep to herself, to stay away from after-work drinks. Wanda shuddered as she thought back to how easily she and the others had criticized that as they drunkenly toasted with beers under a starry Parisian night. Elodie preferred to be home with her kids. What was wrong with that?

"Was it our fault?" she whispered. "Those times when we got on her case for not going out?"

Maddie grasped her hand.

"Goodness, no! This is about what her bosses expected of her: the impossible. They wanted her to leave. She was costing them way too much money with that senior salary, Wanda! For half price, they could get two young ones right out of school. They only keep me around because I have dirt on Louis!"

"A lot has happened since I've been gone."

"That's putting it mildly," Maddie said.

The waiter delivered their lunch, but Wanda had lost her appetite.

❧

As usual, Wanda returned from lunch in less than an hour. With the sadness and shock of Elodie's "accident" looming large, Wanda yearned to plunge herself into one of her favorite tasks: studying the market performance of her companies. The tech guy gave her a thumbs up sign as he passed her in the hallway, an indication that at least she would be able to access her computer.

Thomas Champlain was sitting in her chair, a pile of folders in his lap, as she rounded the corner. Wanda drew in a sharp breath.

"Welcome back!" he exclaimed, popping up from the seat. "Sorry to startle you."

"Thank you. And it's fine. I just wasn't expecting to see someone sitting here."

Thomas shifted the files into her outstretched arms.

"How did things go?" she asked. She tried to sound casual, but she was ready to pounce, ready to criticize him for the blunders she had already imagined.

His face turned almost as red as his hair, but he maintained the smile of superiority that Wanda despised.

"Each fund is down twenty percent."

"What?" Wanda's heart pounded as if it were beating its way out of her chest. Never in her Whilt career had her numbers been that far in the negative. She didn't understand how it was possible. Without trying she could attain better results than that. Most periods, her funds were up eight to ten percent. In a bad period, a fund might dip to negative one percent. But down twenty? How could she justify this to clients? The questions began to multiply in her mind.

"You left me with a bunch of loser stocks, Wanda, so I had to alter a lot of positions." Thomas adjusted his horn-rimmed glasses, and Wanda decided glasses, in fact, did nothing to make one look serious.

"Loser stocks? You mean you sold the positions I'd carefully constructed?"

"They were starting to decline."

"Starting to decline doesn't necessarily mean they will continue to decline!" The look of superiority remained, making Wanda's blood boil. "OK, listen, forget it. I've got to catch up on things."

She turned away but didn't open the files until he disappeared around the corner. Quickly, she grabbed the latest report from her star fund, International Large Cap Prestige, and examined the buys and sells. He sold every share of L'Oreal after the stock slipped four percent in one day on minor news. The shares later gained ten percent. He increased a position in a company she specifically warned him about. Sure, it rose eight percent in one pop, but over the period, it was down fifteen percent.

That idiot! Why couldn't he follow the basic guidelines I gave him?

As her eyes continued to travel through the documents, she found Thomas hadn't followed any of her advice. He had done just the opposite, and as a consequence, ran her funds into the ground.

With a shaky hand, Wanda picked up the phone and began to call her clients.

Chapter 2

When Max Beaumont, diploma fresh in hand, walked out of Wanda's life to join a year-long medical mission in Nigeria, neither of them knew she was pregnant. *No one with an education accidentally gets pregnant these days*, Wanda's mother had scolded. Wanda, as usual, let the remark slide off her back in the weekly telephone conversation that connected her residence in Paris with her parents' home in Boston. So she had taken the pill a few hours—OK, several hours—late. Apparently, that had been enough to make a difference. How was she to know she was that fertile? She was a financial professional, not a doctor.

Max and Wanda had met at an end-of-summer party, and right from that night, Wanda knew he would be leaving for Africa in the coming weeks. But it hadn't stopped either of them. They became a short-term item, and a rather passionate item at that.

She remembered the seductive half-grin, the almond-shaped hazel eyes, the perpetually tousled brown hair. And she remembered the way he made her feel when he looked at her, his eyes never leaving hers each time she spoke. Nothing like her ex, James, whose head always seemed to be buried in his cell phone.

Although a small pang tugged at Wanda's heart every time Max talked about his upcoming trip, she bit her lip and willed a look of strength onto her face. If she stopped him from embarking upon the adventure, any potential relationship was cooked. But, in spite of her efforts to handle the separation as best as she could, she realized a relationship was cooked anyway.

Communication was nearly impossible with difficult access to networks, and Max's schedule was beyond intense. When Wanda found out she was pregnant, she couldn't imagine announcing the news over a crackly phone line as Max prepared for his next life-saving operation. Especially since their phone conversations and emails had been fewer and farther between.

She couldn't blame Max entirely; the situation had become so unbearable that she found herself lashing out at him when they did speak or avoiding his calls altogether. By cutting him out of her life, she regained control.

Not having the baby had only crossed her mind for a few minutes, after Louis' secretary discreetly handed her a piece of paper with the contact details of a doctor who performed abortions at a hospital not far from the office.

She had been taken aback, and her flushed face became contagious, with the bearer of the message hurrying off before Wanda could say a word. Maddie later told her the big bosses hated "losing" their best girls to pregnancy.

"That's ridiculous!" Wanda had said at the time. "If you have a baby, you don't lose brain cells or the desire to do a good job."

"But you might have less time for work and take time for family."

"Many women, and men, have been able to balance both!" Wanda's words came out as defensive even though she knew Maddie wasn't the one she needed to convince.

"Remember Becca from marketing? She sued them for putting her under pressure. Won too. Then disappeared from the world of Whilt."

"How come I never knew about that?" Wanda asked.

"You're too busy working, Wanda. Take a few minutes to open your eyes and observe. You'll see a lot."

Wanda had knitted her brow and looked down at her growing belly. She promised she would extract herself from her bubble from time to time.

Wanda, who had just turned thirty-six, hadn't given much thought one way or the other to having kids. Her relationship with James—her most serious—had lasted five years, but he had always put his career first. Their life had been a string of missed birthdays and evenings out, with Wanda often dining opposite his empty spot at a restaurant table. There was always a good excuse. But in the end, Wanda, no stranger to long hours herself, grew tired of this togetherness that wasn't truly togetherness. They didn't even share an apartment, let alone dreams for a family. The breakup came when James landed a promotion and transfer to London. But Wanda hadn't been sad. The turn of events simply left her relieved. And then, a few months later, Max appeared in her life, and everything changed. A positive change, followed by a negative one: his departure.

Still, much of the positive remained. Wanda saw new possibilities in her life. She no longer accepted stagnation. As the pregnancy progressed past the first weeks, Wanda realized she was getting to like the idea of having this baby—even if it meant doing it alone. Even if it meant a frown from the managers at Whilt.

"You can't be serious about not telling Max!" her best friend Galina had said.

No, she wasn't planning on keeping it a secret

forever, but she didn't see the advantage of tracking him down in Africa. Galina reminded her that he might not ever be back in touch. He might have found someone else and started a new life. Then how would Wanda handle it? Wanda couldn't answer. Her heart ached. Galina, a lawyer, looked at everything with logic, while Wanda looked at everything with emotion.

After three months as a single mother, in spite of the fatigue and stress, Wanda told herself she was satisfied with her life and with her decision—or lack of one. She had stopped thinking of how she would handle the situation. If Max never came back to her, what difference would it make? She'd remembered a few of his comments in passing about not having the time to start a family. Those comments became reassuring, allowing her to justify her silence.

All of these thoughts rushed through her mind as she settled an already sleeping Nelly down in her crib. Nelly, the mirror image of her father with those wide-set hazel eyes. Now they were closed, and their long dark lashes grazed her pink cheeks. The round perfect cheeks that Wanda loved to kiss. She pressed her own cheek against her daughter's and inhaled the soothing, milky scent.

The day might have been terrible for Wanda, but at least for Nelly, everything had gone well. And that was most important. The toddlers loved having a baby around, and the nanny, Colette, said Nelly spent most of her time eyes wide open, eagerly observing her admirers.

Nelly had even smiled for the first time. Wanda's heart ached at missing that moment, yet she knew that with her work schedule she would miss many milestones in the months and years to come. She tried not to think of the "missing" part and instead focused on the "Nelly is happy" part as she tiptoed out of the baby's bedroom and rounded the corner into the living room.

The apartment was cramped, with two minute

bedrooms, a bathroom that required contortionist skills to navigate, and one main room that held a sofa, a small coffee table and an open kitchen that was rudimentary at best. There was one reason the rent was so high: When Wanda sat on the old cream-colored couch with wine stains on it, she looked directly through the bay window at the Eiffel Tower. Galina had a similar view but from a different angle. They would joke around, saying they could wave to each other as they looked out their respective windows.

Wanda ignored the tower's glimmering lights and switched on her laptop. As the clock struck nine, sleep wasn't on her agenda. And neither was amusement. She'd refused the invitation to go out for drinks. She'd refused Galina's invitation for dinner. Wanda decided to avoid her friend because if she saw her in person, she would break down and tell her about the problems at Whilt. And she was sure Galina would put on her attorney cap and say something she wouldn't want to hear.

Nelly was waiting and so was her fund research. She would have to work nights to rebuild the funds Thomas had destroyed. Her clients' words of dissatisfaction rung sharply in her ears once again, and she tried to shut them out. Complaining wouldn't do any good at this point. Only hard work could bring her funds back to performance. But was it too late?

Three days passed before Louis finally waved Wanda inside his office when she approached. Louis ran a hand through the dark hair that fell over his brow and looked up at Wanda through crystal blue eyes that had attitude. He was about Wanda's age and moderately attractive, yet he saw himself as extremely attractive. That was written all over his face, especially when dealing with women. He had been transferred from New York to the Paris office more than a year ago. At first, Wanda had rolled her eyes at his comments, even laughing at his "I'll fuck anyone to get ahead" manner, but after a while she simply avoided him. His behavior had always been borderline—although worse outside the office. But she didn't want to think about that.

She placed her fund reports on the desk, the data facing Louis.

"Thomas should be fired," she said, voice low, confidence high. "This is outrageous. I gave him specific instructions, and he did the opposite."

Louis smiled with what appeared to be feigned sheepishness and shrugged.

"Babe, when you're gone for four months, you can't expect everything to remain frozen. Things evolve."

She flinched. Wanda always flinched when Louis called her "babe," but considering the importance of this conversation, it seemed even more inappropriate than usual.

"In this case, they didn't evolve in the right direction. And I was on maternity leave! I didn't just pop off for a four-month vacation."

Louis stood up and walked around the desk. She refused to step back even though this felt too close for comfort.

"Whatever the reason for the absence, sweetheart, it was an absence."

"It was a normal absence." Wanda's voice trembled with anger. *Control, control, this is all about control*, she reminded herself.

"How about if we discuss this tonight, maybe over a drink?" His lips curved into a smile, and his eyes seemed to undress her. "It's been too long."

Wanda thought back to her only social experience with Louis, the memory she hadn't wanted to stir up: a cocktail hour at a neighborhood bar when she and Max were dating. She'd run into Louis there, and Max had called to cancel after an emergency at the hospital. So they'd had a couple of drinks. But when Louis' hand had ended up wandering up her skirt, her hand had ended up slapping him across the face. The next day at work, business had continued as usual, and Wanda convinced herself to forget about it. He had been drunk. And it had been the first and last such situation.

"Well, what do you say, babe?" he asked, running a finger down her cheek.

She remained frozen to the spot, shocked at his audacity, then took a hasty step back. She hated being on the defensive.

"This is a business matter, Louis, and should be dealt with here in the office," she said, her eyes locking with his.

"I heard you weren't seeing—what is it, Mark?—any more."

"It's Max, but that isn't anyone's business, Louis."

"So you're still saying no to me, sweetheart?" He wore the arrogant smile Wanda knew well.

"Would it make a difference if I said 'yes'?"

"Perhaps. I have power with the powers that be."

Wanda felt as if she'd been hit in the stomach. She wanted to lash out at him, to threaten him, to tell him he wouldn't get away with using her fund performance as a sexual bargaining chip. Instead, she took a deep breath and ordered herself to remain calm, to show indifference.

"Let me say it again: This is a professional matter, and I plan on dealing with it professionally. In the office."

"OK, I'm fine with that."

But it was clear that nothing was fine at all. Wanda's mind was racing. Had Louis set this up from the start, or was he simply taking advantage of an opportunity? In any case, she didn't understand his loyalty to Thomas. He should be punished regardless of whether Wanda was able to salvage the funds.

"Why are you protecting Thomas?" she hissed. "He betrayed me, and he betrayed our clients."

"You only think about business, don't you?" He shook his head and returned to the other side of the desk, where he lounged back in his chair. "This isn't about protecting anyone. It's about being reasonable." Wanda shivered at the chill in his voice, but she didn't waver.

"Being reasonable is handling our clients' money properly. And in this case, that did not happen."

"Well, now that you're back, Wanda, you'll manage to get things in order." All of a sudden, he was businesslike too. Would he have been if she had accepted his advances? Of course not. He'd practically said it himself. She narrowed her eyes and continued as if her boss' outrageous behavior had never happened. She would put it behind her with the barroom memory. But she couldn't put fund performance behind her.

"I can't make any promises, Louis. Did you see these numbers? I know the markets, but I'm not a magician."

"Well maybe you'd better brush up on your tricks." He grinned, as if delighted to see her squirm.

"What do you mean?"

"Wanda, you're experienced enough to be able to iron out this type of problem pretty quickly."

Wanda didn't like the forceful tone of his voice, the implication that she'd better find a solution or else. She especially didn't like this attitude in light of the unpredictable nature of the markets. There weren't guarantees, and Louis knew that as well as she did. So why did he seem adamant about holding her responsible for Thomas' mistakes? Was it punishment for rejecting him?

"When do you expect the funds to return to positive?" she asked. She willed her voice to remain steady and her eyes to remain unafraid, and each obeyed.

"At the end of the quarter."

Not showing an ounce of emotion, she nodded, gathered her papers and left.

Chapter 3

Wanda dressed and undressed and dressed again. She finally settled on a fuzzy khaki-colored sweater-dress that made her eyes look greener and patent leather heels that would give height to her diminutive frame. An outfit she wouldn't wear to work. There. At least she had drawn a line to separate herself from that place. She didn't want to think of Louis, his eyes ripping through her clothing. She slipped a silver strand necklace over her head, and she was good to go.

Colette arrived right on time to watch Nelly, but Wanda still had trouble making it out the door. Nelly was coughing again, wouldn't sleep, wanted to play, didn't want to play… and finally fell asleep.

So at ten-forty-five on the dot, Wanda arrived at the party, now a mass of half-drunken lawyers and their friends spilling over from the main room down the outer staircase. Wanda nodded politely at a few people she knew and continued into the apartment. After years of friendship with Galina and her husband, Charles, Wanda had become acquainted with the attorney crowd.

Still, even if she knew everyone in the room, Wanda

didn't like these big affairs. Discussions were usually meaningless and forgotten by the next day. But it was an excuse to get out—Galina was right, she needed to get out—and she could get by with her usual trick: talking business. She found a few sober acquaintances and did just that. She'd scanned the room but hadn't seen Galina. She did spot Charles though, caught up in conversation in a far corner, so she would stumble upon her friend at some point. *If* she decided to stay.

Two glasses of champagne later, the bubbles having gone a bit to her head, Wanda did a double take as a familiar figure in the doorway caught her eye. Suitcase in hand, unshaven and exhausted, he made his way past the group lingering in the vestibule. Wanda squinted to be sure she wasn't imagining things. But in her heart she knew she wasn't. She felt his presence. Max. He was back. And from the way it looked, he was staying here.

Her first thought was panic, her second thought was anger (had Galina set this up?), then she forgot about the panic and anger, and tried to figure out what was happening.

She excused herself mid-conversation and hurried out to the terrace, nearly empty as guests realized the Paris autumn was turning to winter. Wanda glanced around, seeking Galina, but she was nowhere to be found. *Damn!*

Wanda ran through the situation: A lawyer-doctor couple lived in the apartment. They were about her age so it was possible the doctor knew Max from medical school or residency. A year had passed since Max's departure. He had fulfilled his promise of a year-long mission. Wanda ignored the flip-flopping of her heart. She lingered near the sliding glass door until she was certain there was a clear path to the front door. Then she bolted.

Tears streamed down her face as she hurried through

the streets. She didn't take the subway or a cab, but instead she threaded through cobblestone side streets until she was on a main avenue that would lead her home. She would rather walk all night than settle into the confinements of a car or subway. The tears continued, and she didn't wipe them away. So much of her wanted to run into Max's arms, but now, after her year of unconventional decisions, she didn't know how.

و‿و

It was two a.m., but Wanda felt more comfortable in the glaring light of her laptop than in her bed. Poring over corporate balance sheets was the only way to get her mind off her almost-encounter with Max. A half hour later, she was fully immersed, smiling into her own reflection on the screen as she noted useful details about a particular company's outlook. On Monday, she would increase her position in this one.

Her cell phone vibrated at her side, startling her, and Galina's name flashed on the screen.

"What is it?" she asked distractedly after popping in the earpiece. She and Galina called each other at any hour, so this wasn't a surprise. As images of the evening rushed back to her, she had plenty of questions she wanted to ask. But Galina was already speaking.

"Why did you run out?"

"You saw me? Where were you? I looked everywhere for you, Galina!"

"Of course I saw you. You almost crashed right into me!"

Wanda had been running blindly, only thinking of escape. If she had crossed her best friend or anyone else, she wouldn't have known the difference.

"Did anyone… else… notice me?

"If you're referring to Max, no. He'd already

disappeared into one of the bedrooms, and that was the last I saw of him."

"What was he doing there? Did you know?"

"Of course not! I'm not one to play games, Wanda. I shouldn't have to tell you that after all these years."

Wanda felt overheated suddenly, and her heart pounded into her eardrums. This reaction, and she wasn't even facing Max. The rush of emotion scared her, worried her.

"It turns out he's friends with Rich," Galina said. "They went to med school together. Max is in Paris for two days, something work-related."

Wanda's heart sank. He wasn't back after all. Forty-eight hours and he would once again be thousands of miles away. She scolded herself for her sentimentality. She had been doing so well these past months, and now here she was, disappointed like a lovesick teenager.

"It doesn't matter anyway." She hoped her voice sounded proud rather than pathetic, even though she realized pulling one over on Galina was impossible. At times, her friend knew her better than she knew herself.

"Two days is plenty of time for you to tell him about Nelly," Galina said quietly.

"No. Not now."

"Wanda, timing won't ever be right if it's up to you."

Wanda remained silent, unmoving. She refused to budge. If Max chose to knock on her door, she would bring up the subject. Otherwise, it was out of the question.

"Why couldn't I find you?" Wanda asked, changing the subject. "Where were you hiding out?"

"I was busy talking to one of the interns from Charles' firm. I kept an eye out for you, but with the size of the crowd we must have just missed each other. And then I convinced myself that you hadn't come after all, that you'd stayed home with your friend the computer."

"I wish I'd stayed home."
"You can't keep running away, Wanda."
And she knew her friend was right.

Chapter 4

Nelly snuggled her warm head against her mother's chest and reached little fingers out to grasp whatever they could. Wanda moved about the apartment with the baby carrier strapped to her, and both mom and daughter were satisfied. Wanda brushed a hand over the soft, curly blond hair that was beginning to thicken. Nelly cooed and gurgled, a cute little after-breakfast symphony that soothed Wanda before she headed off to work. Moments later, she handed this little bundle off to Colette and tried to ignore the pain in her heart as she raced down the stairs for another ten-hour day.

Wanda's morning was a series of out-of-office meetings with furious clients.

"How could the company let this happen?"

"What sort of fuck-up was left with that much control over our money?"

"How can you possibly bring these funds back with the market in such a catastrophic state?"

The questions went on and on, and Wanda tried to stem the concern, and in some cases, wrath.

At least the turmoil kept her mind off the fact that

the rest of the weekend had gone by, along with most of the week, with no word from Max. She had been right not to contact him. If she was indeed so important to him, he would have tried to reach out.

Finally, back to the office in the middle of lunch hour, Wanda had to set up a conference room for her next meeting before she could even consider stuffing something into her mouth. She smoothed back a few locks of hair that had escaped from her chignon as she glanced at her reflection in the many windows lining the hall. She felt frazzled and looked it too.

A few more steps and round the corner. Wanda shivered as she passed the room that remained taped up since Elodie's fatal fall. She hated even approaching the area, but she would have to get over it. She worked here and had to use the conference rooms.

Wanda was about to enter the next conference room when she stopped in her tracks. Louis' voice rang out. Everyone knew those rooms were so poorly insulated that even a whisper could be heard in the hallway, but Louis never seemed to care. He was brazen when it came to just about everything.

"You want me to change her old performance evaluation? Yeah, I know it looks bad she was put on probation and then jumped to her death—but how the hell can anyone prove we're responsible?"

Silence. He was on the phone with someone. Wanda remained frozen to the spot. After a minute she gasped, realizing she hadn't been breathing.

"OK, OK, fine, as long as HR backs this up, I'll sign whatever damn evaluation you need me to sign… When do you need the paperwork?"

As Louis wrapped up the conversation, Wanda hurried back around the corner and lingered at the water cooler, her head buried in her pile of folders. Louis walked past, nodding at her curtly, and she looked up to call out a faint greeting, as if she had been lost in her analyses.

She knew what she had heard. A big cover up to avoid responsibility for what had happened to Elodie.

Nothing about the situation seemed right. First of all, Elodie had been one of the most efficient long-term employees at Whilt. How could the company put her on probation? And now altering her performance evaluation to escape responsibility… "Inappropriate" wasn't strong enough to express what was happening right under her nose.

You should say something! Wanda told herself. Then she thought better of it. She didn't have an ounce of proof. What did her words mean against those of a major corporation? And it wasn't her business anyway.

Wanda returned to her desk as if the events of a few minutes ago hadn't occurred. But deep down, she couldn't forget.

༄༅

Flora leaned against the edge of Wanda's desk. Her ginger-colored hair fell over one shoulder to her waist, and she toyed with the edges of it as she spoke. She had been begging Wanda to join her, Sam and a few others for drinks. "The usual routine," she said with a shrug.

But it hadn't been Wanda's usual routine for months, and now, with Nelly waiting for her, she couldn't bear the thought of getting home even later.

"It's not like I'm the life of the party," Wanda said, rolling her eyes as she swiveled around in her chair. "So what if I don't come out with you tonight?"

"You've refused us every time since you've been back, Wanda! You stay here late, then run home. Same thing every day."

"Have you seen the fund performance Thomas left

me with?"

"Look, I know, you told me." Flora sighed. "But you can't work twenty-four-seven. And you can't restrict your life to work duty and mom duty and nothing else."

Wanda covered her face with her hands and shook her head.

"OK, fine," she said, her voice muffled. "I'll go, but just for a half hour. I can't have the nanny doing overtime until midnight."

"Perfect!" Flora reached over Wanda and clicked the mouse to shut down Wanda's computer.

"Luckily I already saved my files," Wanda said, grabbing her coat as Flora smiled mischievously.

They met the others at the Irish pub around the block. Together, the two women squeezed past the rowdy crowd in front to the booths in the back. Sam ordered beers for everyone except Wanda, who hated beer and stuck to a glass of red wine.

"Finally," Sam said, touching his glass to hers. "Welcome back, Wanda. So you haven't abandoned a social life after all..." He grinned and took a swig of beer. And then the usual conversation, a rehashing of the workday, the gossip from other Whilt offices or clients. Wanda watched the excitement in their eyes as they chatted about this and that. Had she really been a part of it all only a few months ago? Yes. She remembered it clearly. She remembered being that excited about the latest goings-on in the office. And now, she could only glance at the time ticking forward on her watch and think of those extra minutes not spent by Nelly's side.

"You're quiet, Wanda," Sam said. "Still thinking of your funds?"

"You would be too if you were in my position."

"Yeah, word has made its way around the office."

"I'm sure it has."

"Thomas is such a goddamn idiot," Flora said. "The

situation sucks."

"I don't understand why Louis is protecting him." Wanda took a sip of wine, savoring the sensations on her tongue. This was her second drink since having Nelly. The first had been a sip of champagne with Galina and Charles on her first day back from the hospital.

"It's simple, darling," Sam said. "Don't you know Thomas is a cousin of one of the bigwigs in New York?"

"That would explain it," Wanda said. The news didn't surprise her. She couldn't imagine Louis protecting such a person without a motive. Louis didn't do much of anything for free.

Conversation moved on to Sam's holiday plans, and after a short time of pretending to listen, Wanda slid out of the booth and dropped a bill on the table.

"So soon?" Sam asked.

"I've got a baby waiting."

Chapter 5

"Mom, I'm sorry, I'm not going to be anywhere near Boston," Wanda said, phone to ear as she pushed through the revolving doors of the tower on Madison Avenue. "I'm here for three days on business... No, it's not a good idea if you come down... I'll be in the office most of the time."

But the real reason Wanda didn't want her mother to hop on the next plane to New York was because of what her mother would see in her daughter's eyes. It would take her about three seconds to realize something was wrong. Daily phone calls would ensue, along with pleas for Wanda to move back home, into her old room, and go to work at her cousin's accounting firm. Wanda shuddered at the thought. She loved her mother, and smiled at memories of afternoons together watching movies or strolling around Harvard Square, but she needed space. Her mother never could understand this need and often equated it with coldness—but Wanda wasn't cold. She was simply a bit of a loner at times.

Wanda wrapped up the conversation as she headed for the elevator bank. She hadn't been to the "snake pit" in two years, but nothing much had changed. The gorgeous glass tower was still a vile place, with the tension in the air thick and pervasive. She remembered her way to Raymond Grant's office. Yet another member of management overseeing her work without seeing it at all.

She checked her appearance in the mirrored elevator as it whisked her to the sixth floor. Tweed suit not too rumpled, green silk scarf properly tied. At least those small efforts might compensate for the bloodshot eyes and puffy lids after a long and restless flight.

As a matter of fact, she hadn't gotten much sleep since Louis told her she would be traveling to New York in exactly thirty-six hours to discuss the future of her funds. Was that positive or negative? Impossible to read on Louis' poker face, and she wouldn't give him the satisfaction of seeing her concern. She'd tried not to think about what would unfold in New York and focused on preparing Nelly for her stay with Galina and Charles. The drop-off had been a teary one, another reason for Wanda's red eyes and sleeplessness.

A booming voice broke into her thoughts. Anyone would expect an impressive figure attached to that voice, but Raymond Grant was rather round and unassuming in appearance. He was balding and wore glasses that magnified his blue eyes. His shirt was always untucked or not quite the right size, giving him a disheveled look. Those who crossed him in the street probably wouldn't give him a second glance, would never guess he wielded such power.

Raymond Grant's reign was one of terror. Because anyone who hoped to climb the corporate ladder had better please him. And Raymond was not easy to please. Raymond greeted Wanda, kissing her on both cheeks the European way, and led her into his office as if they were on an important secret mission together.

"First things first, Wendy," he said.

"It's Wanda."

But he didn't seem to notice the correction as he settled down behind his desk. Two of the buttons on his shirt looked as if they might pop at any second as the bright blue material stretched across his belly.

He slid a key ring toward Wanda.

"What's this?" she asked.

"My wife and I won't be in our apartment for the next few days, so you can stay in the guest room. Let yourself in, make yourself at home."

"But I thought I would be staying at the Plaza. I had to fill out all that travel paperwork." Suspicion filled Wanda's mind. A room was ready and waiting at the Plaza, Whilt's swanky hotel of choice. She knew that, because upon arrival, she'd called to verify the check-in time. So the question was, *Who would be staying there?*

"Never mind the details, you'll be more than comfortable in our home. It's much more personal, unlike the cold feeling of a hotel. Now let's get down to business."

Wanda tried to push the strange start to the conversation out of her mind as Raymond stared at her across the heavy mahogany desk that didn't match the modernity of the rest of the decor.

"We want to expand the reach of our funds. Today, it's all about Asia, and at the moment, we're losing ground over there. We need to offer more to our clients in China, Japan…"

Wanda felt her heart thumping, a combination of relief and fear. Raymond hadn't yet mentioned her recent fund performance, but that didn't mean he didn't have something worse planned to discuss.

"As of next week, you will be expanding your international fund to include Asian companies, and you also will take on the management of another Asian fund established through our office in Shanghai."

Wanda hesitated long enough to digest this indigestible information but not long enough to lose the nerve to speak out.

"But that makes no sense. I've built an expertise in Western European countries; I'm familiar with their management styles and know the CEOs. With Asia, I would have to start from scratch. That would be fine if I didn't already have four other funds to manage!"

"Are you saying this is too much for you?"

"I'm saying it isn't logical—not when others in the office only manage two funds. Are you planning on paying me a second salary for taking on this second job of sorts?"

"Considering the performance of your current funds, no."

Wanda wanted to burst out with something sarcastic, something rebellious, but the words remained captive in her throat. She rarely fell silent after what she considered an injustice; usually her emotions won out. But this time was different. She was in a state of disbelief. Her mind was racing. Was this punishment, stemming from her rejection of Louis? No, he didn't wield that much power. But he probably did all he could to push her into a difficult position.

"You'll have to fly to Shanghai next week. CEOs of the biggest Asian companies will be at a conference there. A perfect opportunity for you to do some research."

Wanda knew about the conference since one of her colleagues, who was based in Shanghai, attended each year. If she hadn't been suspicious of Raymond's intentions, she actually would have been excited about the opportunity. But somehow, with her other funds suffering, and the learning curve this new endeavor required, this didn't seem like an opportunity. This seemed like a map to lead her down the road to failure.

❦

Wanda had been so absorbed in her analyses at the guest desk near the window, that at first, she hadn't heard the commotion. And it wasn't really "commotion" when it started. Just a bit of giggling, then some whispering. Wanda sat in the far corner of the sixteenth floor, her desk pressed against the glass so if she looked down for too long, she just might shiver. Wanda was afraid of heights. But that wasn't a problem because she didn't have time to watch the passersby with their coffee cups and cell phones. When Wanda was at work, she worked.

But now she was thirsty, and so she headed to the cafeteria. As she crossed the room, she noticed smiles here and there, looks of concern, people chatting in low voices. It was as if everyone was trying to look inconspicuous, yet that made them stand out all the more. They didn't seem to notice Wanda so whatever was going on didn't have anything to do with her. She shook her head and rounded the corner. And that's when she heard it, coming from one level below.

Someone was singing *Singing in the Rain*. In a rich, deep voice, loud enough to carry through the open space cutting through each floor from the atrium to the roof.

Wanda took the elevator down a flight and arrived in time to see a man she recognized but didn't know by name dancing through the planters, his loafers kicking up dirt and glossy beads. The look on his face was not one of joy but of delirium.

Before she even had a chance to ask one of the other employees what was happening, security guards had already whisked the man off, and like scurrying mice, the onlookers dispersed.

Wanda remained in front of the elevator bank, staring

at the splotches of dirt on the tile, and only came out of her fog when a hand touched hers. Tricia Warren. One of the analysts who used to work in the Paris office.

"Did you see that?" Wanda hissed as Tricia kissed her on both cheeks.

"Oh you mean Jim Tuxford?" She rolled her eyes. "Management drove him crazy. Par for the course, huh?"

And then she slipped into the ascending elevator before Wanda could reply.

Chapter 6

Wanda looked out the window at the city lights and shivered. More than the heights made her quake in this place. Raymond's apartment was cold and impersonal, with stark white walls, a few generic abstract paintings in reds and yellows, and sparse furnishings. She was sure the Plaza would have been much warmer and more welcoming than this place.

She sank onto the black leather couch with a sigh and looked around. Did a couple in their fifties live here, and had they raised a child here? It felt more like a modern art museum than a home. Everything was in perfect order. The housekeeper Wanda had crossed on her way in clearly did an exemplary job. The only splash of personality in the whole place was a stack of playbills on the glass coffee table. Raymond and his wife were theater fans. But wouldn't anyone with a big corporate salary in New York City be a Broadway patron? Wanda snorted, finding it hard to imagine Raymond smiling and clapping about anything. Maybe his wife was the theater lover, and he went along to please her. Wanda snorted again, finding it hard to imagine Raymond trying to please anyone.

She made every effort to occupy herself, switching on and off the TV, then the radio, then answering emails on her phone. But whenever she returned to reality, the shroud of heaviness remained.

The clock struck nine. She thought of changing into her pajamas, settling into bed in the black and white room down the hall, closing her eyes in this silent place. This would be repeated three times, for her three-night stay. And right then and there, she knew she couldn't do it.

༄

An hour later, Wanda and Tricia were sipping martinis at a bar in the East Village. A casual place with cozy booths, brick walls and low lighting a block away from Tricia's apartment. Wanda had taken her up on her invitation and would be spending three nights on the pull-out couch.

"The cleaning lady told me 'Mrs. Raymond' was on a trip to visit family, so I don't understand what Raymond is doing, leaving me his apartment in the middle of the workweek when he is indeed in town and in the office."

"Dear Wanda," Tricia said, shaking her head so that her long auburn ponytail swung over one shoulder, "you haven't been around these people enough. Raymond has done this before. You expense the hotel tab for Raymond and his girlfriend. He so kindly leaves you his apartment in return."

"Are you kidding me?" Wanda didn't consider herself to be particularly naïve, but apparently, she was when faced with the goings-on at Whilt. She felt her face go hot, ashamed she hadn't seen through such a sham.

"Don't feel bad about not realizing it," Tricia said, as if reading her mind. "The people running the show are pretty unbelievable."

"But are you sure this is what's going on? It's not just a rumor?"

"It's the sad truth. I have my sources."

"Seriously?" Wanda took a sip of her martini, savoring the cool bitterness. She felt like drowning herself in a dozen before returning to that place in the morning.

"Seriously," Tricia said. "Raymond probably doesn't even care if the underlings know. That's the way it is at Whilt—like it or fuck off."

"Why do you put up with it?" Wanda asked.

"I could ask you the same."

"I'm just discovering this side of the company."

Tricia smirked. "I put up with it because when you know how to manipulate them, you can climb your way to the top."

"You've tried?" Wanda couldn't mask the sarcasm in her voice.

Tricia leaned closer. "Can you keep a secret?"

"Of course!" Wanda, usually indifferent to gossip, suddenly found herself yearning to pull the words from Tricia's mouth.

"I fucked my way to lower management level, where I am now, with someone you know very well. Louis, your fearless Parisian leader."

Should I be surprised? Wanda thought as her eyes widened. After Louis' behavior, probably not.

"It got me out of that shitty analyst job. And at least Louis is pretty hot. Not a bad deal." She grinned and took a sip of her drink. Wanda noticed the assortment of rocks on her fingers. Tricia might have a small apartment, but she was living the high life in other ways.

"Tricia, you're smart enough to get far with your skills! Why resort to that?" The words sounded dull and naïve, but Wanda couldn't stop herself from saying them.

Wanda didn't know if she was angry with Tricia or disappointed with her. Perhaps a bit of both.

Tricia sighed. "You're right. Of course, you're right. But that isn't how Whilt operates. And it's how so many others do business too. This isn't about Whilt alone. What's a girl to do?"

"But Tricia, don't you realize what your actions mean for the rest of us women?" Wanda couldn't hold back the exasperation in her voice.

Tricia shook her head and reached across the table for Wanda's hand. "Listen, I know... I do feel guilty sometimes. I'm not proud of this. But dammit, Wanda, do you see anyone else who will look out for me and help me move up the corporate ladder? I'd like to be able to afford something better than a teeny-tiny walkup some day! It's the same everywhere. I'm simply working with the system instead of fighting it. Not everyone has the courage to fight."

Wanda glimpsed a hint of sadness in Tricia's eyes and softened. Tricia's decisions weren't any of her business. *And who knows how any of us would react in a given situation?*

Wanda didn't dare ask Tricia if she was still using her strategy to make it to upper management. She just wanted to get on the next plane out of this city. But that wish would have to wait.

"So do you hate me?" Tricia asked, trying—but failing—to be flippant.

"I don't agree with you, but no, I don't hate you. I do think you're selling yourself short, though."

Tricia smiled wistfully, then shook her head, and the fragility was gone.

"So how are things in Paris?" she asked.

"Fine."

"And my ex hasn't tried to jump you?"

"What makes you say that?"

"Hmm, so he is up to his old tricks—"

"No, no, I just didn't get why you were asking me. I'm back from maternity leave after all. It's not like I'm the best candidate for dating. Most people would assume I'm with someone anyway."

"Ha! That wouldn't bother Louis. As long as you've got a nice ass, Louis is interested."

"Well thanks for the compliment," Wanda said, irony in her voice.

Tricia laughed.

"As long as he's treating you well, and things are going OK, I'm happy, Wanda. I learned a lot from you back in the Paris office. You deserve to be successful. And that's damn difficult for women at this company. It doesn't help if you're a mother and making what they consider the big bucks. It also doesn't help if you refuse to drink the Kool-Aid." At this, she smirked and downed the rest of her drink.

Wanda's mind raced as she thought of her own situation: An over-thirty mother making one of the highest salaries in the Paris office. She hadn't told Tricia of her troubles, hadn't dared to pronounce the words aloud, hadn't dared to consider herself a victim. She didn't want to be a victim, but facing this situation, how could she be anything else?

She took another sip—this time a gulp—of her drink, steeled herself and leaned closer to Tricia. Wanda knew what she had to do on this trip. She had to gather as much information, as much insight as she possibly could. She had a feeling it would serve her well.

"What really happened with Jim today? That singing in the planters thing. He's one of the top guys, right under Raymond."

"Raymond's hated him from the start." Tricia rolled her eyes as if she'd told the story every day of her life. "For years, Raymond's put on a show of solidarity for the outside world, but behind the scenes, he's made Jim's life hell. Jim hadn't been in the office for a few days, and then he showed up as Gene Kelly! That'll be the 'underground' talk of the office for the next few days. Management will brush it under the rug though. Remember: It never happened."

"Is it always like this around here? It's overwhelming."

Tricia laughed and shook her head. "It is pretty dysfunctional, isn't it?"

"So I'm not overreacting, not being overly serious? I can be overly serious."

"I know. We worked together, remember?" Tricia grinned, and so did Wanda.

But as Wanda laughed and meandered into more pleasant subjects, the knot in her stomach remained.

Chapter 7

Galina hugged Wanda, who was already cradling Nelly in her arms. Nelly had smiled and giggled as soon as she saw her mother and then grasped the buttons of Wanda's shirt with eager fingers. A joyous reunion that made Wanda's hear soar.

Wanda followed her friend's tall willowy silhouette into the living room, where she'd prepared tea. Everyone admired Galina for her beauty—a combination of Russian and Nigerian genes that resulted in cocoa-colored skin and golden eyes—and her brain—a list of degrees and awards that resulted in a position at a top law firm. But Wanda admired Galina for her loyalty. Friends since freshman year of college, together they'd been through failed exams and failed relationships, lost and seized opportunities, and even an international move. In college, they'd set their sights on Paris and managed to land jobs within six months of each other.

Wanda held Nelly against her chest, feeling the baby's heart beating against her own. Its rapid rhythm seemed to pound right through Wanda's body. A tear slipped from the corner of her eye, but she brushed it away. She was being too emotional, as usual. She'd only been away for three days, yet it had felt more like three weeks. Nelly snuggled against her neck, drooling into her hair.

"Here," Galina said, laughing as she handed her a burp cloth. "I think she's working on a tooth."

"Already? It seems kind of soon!"

"Anya had her first at four months," Galina said, referring to her four-year-old daughter.

Wanda sank onto the cool leather couch and gazed out the window. The Eiffel Tower by day, and her apartment in the distance.

"I sometimes feel like I can wave to you," she said to Galina.

"You always say that." Galina grinned, set cups on the table and poured fragrant Earl Grey. "So much so, that I can't look out the window without thinking of you. So… how did things go? Not all rosy, huh?"

Galina sat cross legged in one corner of the couch, her elegant beige tunic fanning out around her.

Wanda felt her face go red. She still didn't want to share the turmoil of the past few weeks with Galina. This was unlike her and unlike what usually happened in their friendship. Maybe it was because she knew what Galina would say, those words Wanda herself had whispered, then tried to bury in the depths of her mind. Words like *sexual harassment, discrimination* and *lawsuit*. Galina was all about taking action. Wanda was all about avoiding it.

"It's just the workload," Wanda said vaguely. "They gave me some Asian funds to manage, and I have to leave for Shanghai next week. For a week. Can you watch Nelly again?" Her words ran together in an attempt to sound blasé, but in her own ears, she sounded more distraught than anything else.

Galina took a sip of tea as Wanda placed a fussing Nelly in the baby lounger and started bouncing it with her foot. Wanda drowned her gaze in her cup of tea, a sad attempt at ignoring Galina's quizzical and knowing eye.

"Of course we can watch Nelly. That's never a problem. But Wanda, this fund story... Did they offer you a promotion or a raise? A new contract?"

"No."

"So you've got the funds you're already managing, plus the new ones, and nothing official to document the change."

"That's about right."

"Well, the problem is that *isn't* right."

Wanda rolled her eyes and sipped her tea as if it were a drug, easing her discomfort. She glanced down at Nelly, who chewed on the ear of her elephant toy. *It is a tooth*, she thought as she watched Nelly smile through the drool. Then she snapped back to attention at the sound of her friend's voice.

"This is serious, Wanda. If you give them an inch, they'll take a yard. Believe me."

Wanda could trust her friend, whose legal specialty was defending companies involved in labor disputes.

"I know their tricks, their motivations," Galina continued.

This would be the perfect time to tell Galina everything, from the day Wanda returned to the office from maternity leave to now. But she couldn't. The words remained trapped in her throat.

"Don't tell me it's already time to send little Nelly home?" Charles' voice echoed from the vestibule. His first stop was Galina, naturally. He dropped to his knees at her side and drew her into his arms, then kissed her gently on the forehead.

They had been married for five years, but they were still in honeymoon mode. On a physical level, the opposites-attract magnetism hadn't waned. Charles was a freckly, light-skinned, green-eyed Frenchman from a family that traced its way back—accurately or not was still to be determined—to aristocracy. A contrast to Galina's dark beauty. And on an intellectual level, their similarities were what kept the fire ignited. Attorneys at the same firm, they had worked on a case together, and in the process, fallen in love.

Charles approached Wanda and kissed her on both cheeks. He was a brotherly figure for her, and she was convinced he felt sorry for her much of the time. When Galina could be a little too straightforward, he would temper his wife's words and pat Wanda on the back. She didn't know if she was grateful for his kindness or embarrassed about being pathetic enough to need it.

Galina poured Charles a cup of tea even though it was cocktail hour rather than teatime and told him about Wanda's new assignments. But this wasn't an exercise in casual chitchat. Wanda knew her too well. Galina was hoping to gain an ally, someone to help her convince Wanda that she had to speak out at work.

"I know Galina considers it her business," he said with a grin, "but I realize it isn't any of mine, Wanda. Your decisions have to be your own. And you haven't asked for my advice, so I feel uncomfortable giving it."

"Charles! We can't let her head straight into a disaster." Galina shook her head. "We know better. It's our responsibility to—"

"Galina, don't worry, OK?" Wanda said. "Please stop talking about me as if I weren't here."

"You expect me not to worry just because you tell me not to worry? That's not logical, Wanda."

Wanda sighed. Of course it wasn't logical.

Charles set a hand on Wanda's wrist and spoke in his usual calm manner. "If you were to ask for advice, I would agree with Galina. The law is the law. But when you insist the law be followed, that action comes with consequences."

"I'm not ready for the consequences."

"That's what they're betting on," Galina muttered.

And Wanda knew her friend was right. She thought of all she hadn't told Galina and Charles. Whilt was truly counting on the fact that Wanda and her colleagues would accept anything—anything to avoid conflict.

Chapter 8

Wanda had been to Shanghai once before for Whilt business, meeting with fund managers Rita Morelle and Xavier Laval, who had originally worked in Paris and handed off the European funds to her. That had been several years ago, in the middle of summer when the air was steamy, and ladies walked around in flip flops and short dresses.

This time, it was winter, darker and cooler. Wanda stayed at an elegant, modern hotel, with dozens of stories piercing through the sky. It was a calm, quiet place, perfect after long, intense days at the conference. She interviewed chief executive after chief executive, grilled financial officers with questions, met with analysts and yawned her way through formal presentations that never brought forth the real dirt. With each meeting, she emerged with a boost of energy that buoyed her confidence. *I can do this*, she thought. She could apply much of her experience from the European market, then integrate the new elements unique to Asia.

That is why she agreed to dinner with Rita and Xavier rather than holing up in her room with a bowl of noodles and the television. Wanda, for the first time in weeks, felt as if maybe, just maybe, everything would be all right. She would build up these funds and prove to management that they couldn't keep her down.

Wanda met Rita and Xavier in the lobby lounge, near the pianist playing Gershwin's best.

"Very New York, tonight," Xavier said with a grin as he kissed Wanda on both cheeks. Rita arrived in a flourish of red, her silk dress flying around her.

"Our arrival was almost simultaneous," she said, glancing at Xavier. The two were a discreet item, with no one in the office officially aware of the situation. They were in their early fifties, but looked a decade younger in that breezy French sort of way.

"How's the conference going?" Xavier asked. "You've been like a gust of wind, in and out of the office before anyone can say more than 'hello.'"

Wanda pressed her hands to her temples and shook her head.

"Overwhelming. But good."

"I can't believe they're giving you the Asian funds too," Rita said, rubbing Wanda's arm. "That's insane. Are you sure you're up for this, Wanda? I know you can do a fabulous job, but with this, your other funds and your home life, how are you going to balance everything? You know Whilt will eat you up and doesn't care if your personal life suffers."

Rita was direct, but her words were always kind, meant to help, not hurt.

"I still haven't figured that out yet," Wanda said. "I'm at the stage of plowing ahead like a good little Whilt soldier."

"They love that," Xavier said, then signaled the waiter. "What would everyone like for dinner?"

They settled on tea and various rolls and noodles.

"So, what have you been working on?" Wanda asked.

Xavier and Rita exchanged glances. Wanda raised an eyebrow and leaned closer.

"C'mon, guys, we've known each other long enough."

Rita nodded at Xavier, and he sighed.

"OK, I think we both realize we have to tell you this, especially since you're building a fund of Asian companies. As you can probably guess, Rita and I have many contacts throughout the region after our years over here. One of them recently leaked some information to us, and as it turns out, it's true."

"What is it?" Wanda asked.

The waiter arrived with tea, and Wanda grudgingly thanked him. She was too eager to hear what Xavier had to reveal.

"You know I split my time between the Shanghai and Tokyo offices. Well, my source told me about a Japanese company that is illegally betting on bitcoins," Xavier said.

"What does that have to do with our business?" Wanda asked. "Unless your funds have been investing in that company."

"Oh, it's worse than that," Xavier said with a smirk. "One of Whilt's biggest private clients is that company's CEO."

"What?" Wanda almost choked on a sip of tea. "Oh no."

"Oh yes," Rita said, nodding.

"So we're investing illegal money?"

"More or less," Xavier said with a grin. "Or at least, I am. I manage his money out of the Tokyo office. A certain Mr. Ito pours all his money into my Eastern Development fund, upon my suggestion of course."

"What are you going to do?" Wanda managed to cobble a few words together. "Have you told anyone? Management, I mean."

"I told the higher ups in New York, and as I

suspected, they want me to pretend I've never heard a thing. To keep on investing Ito's money. They don't want a scandal, and they certainly don't want to lose Ito. Remember: Never piss off a client. Especially a major client like this one."

"You're kidding."

The waiter arrived, setting a selection of steaming plates on the table in one quick swoop. Xavier grabbed a shrimp roll, dunked it into a tangerine-colored sauce and looked at Wanda. His expression had gone from whimsical to grim.

"I'm afraid not," he replied.

"We're telling you for one reason," Rita said. "If Ito approaches you, or if they try to hand him over to you, think of this before you decide to invest his money."

"But why would that happen? If he's Xavier's client…"

And then she understood. She looked from Xavier to Rita. Their eyes were opaque, hiding the distress that must have been percolating beneath the surface.

Xavier knew too much. Xavier wouldn't bend to pressure. Xavier was going to lose his job.

∽◇∾

Xavier and Rita turned the conversation to other subjects, but the night was ruined for Wanda. It sickened her that Xavier would be fired for doing the right—the legal—thing, and Whilt would cover it up. Wanda cut the evening short, blaming fatigue, but she tossed and turned most of the night in that oversized bed with heavy down pillows.

In the morning, she felt drugged as she dragged herself out of her room and into the frigid air, a messily packed suitcase at her side. She handed the taxi driver a small card with the address of Whilt written in Mandarin, then settled against the seat as the car drove the short distance.

The small office, as usual, was buzzing with activity as Wanda entered, filled up on coffee in the kitchen, and slouched behind the guest desk. In exactly five hours, she would be heading to the airport and back to Paris. Normally, she would be jumping out of her skin with excitement at the thought of returning home, holding Nelly, seeing Galina. But a strange sense of foreboding— one that had begun in the Paris office and had been growing since—had reached colossal proportions after her conversation with Xavier and Rita.

Wanda brooded into her coffee mug as she scanned the pitiful performance of her funds and thought of all of the ways she would love to punish Thomas Champlain for ruining her portfolio. And her life.

She hadn't seen Xavier arrive, but all of a sudden, she heard his voice, whispering angrily with another colleague. She recognized it as Albert, Xavier's associate. They were hidden by a partition on one side of Wanda's desk.

"You can't be serious!" Albert said.

"Ask the reporter," Xavier said. "He can assure you that I'm indeed serious." Wanda could tell he was grinning as he pronounced those words.

"But they're going to can you if the story comes out!"

"Al, don't tell me you're that naïve. They're going to fire me anyway."

"Then why haven't they done it? You told them about Ito weeks ago."

"I'm sure they have their reasons," Xavier said, his voice cool, unbothered by Al's hysteria.

So Xavier had spoken to the press, Albert thought he shouldn't have—and who the hell knew when this whole story was going to explode? Wanda jumped, the papers spread across her keyboard spilling into her lap and onto the floor.

"I didn't mean to startle." The receptionist, a young Chinese woman with lovely but halting English. "I wonder what time you like me to schedule cab?"

"Cab?"

"You leave today, yes?"

Wanda nodded and hastily gathered her papers. The receptionist's heavy veil of black hair fell over one shoulder as she looked at her notebook.

"Four o'clock?" she asked.

"Yes, yes, the flight is at four."

"You leave one o'clock. I call for you."

"OK, thanks," Wanda said as the woman returned to her desk.

She turned back to her computer and listened for the men's voices. But all had fallen silent.

Chapter 9

"Wanda, we're not going to make it for Hanukkah-Christmas," her mother said as soon as Wanda answered the phone.

Life in Paris had resumed, with all thoughts of Wanda's adventures in New York and China pushed to the back of her mind as she tried to catch up on hugs with Nelly, mountains of laundry and mounds of paperwork.

"I tried, I really tried," her mother muttered. "But it's impossible. We're going to be stuck at home for the holidays."

Wanda's mother was Jewish, and her father was Catholic, of French origin. Even though that made Wanda officially Jewish, "officially" she didn't practice much of anything. But the family tradition was to celebrate both holidays.

This year, however, she didn't feel like celebrating, so her mother's news came as a relief. She was less relieved to learn her father had broken his leg, though—the reason for the trip's cancellation.

"It's a mess over here, Wanda." She could see her

mother shaking her head as she ran through the house, tackling ten tasks at once. "The airline, the insurers… All asking for dozens of papers. Your father can't do a thing on his own. He's driving me crazy. And that's not the half of it."

Wanda decided this was the perfect excuse for lying if and when her mother asked, "How's work?" or "How did the New York trip go?" But the conversation wasn't moving in that direction.

"How about you come home for the holidays, Wanda?" her mother asked. "It's been a while since you've spent them in Boston. We'll pay for your ticket."

"Mom, I can afford a plane ticket." Wanda sighed, loudly enough to be heard over a transatlantic phone line. "But thank you."

"So you'll come?"

"I can't. Work has been piling up. You know I'm just back from maternity leave."

"They won't let you take time off, so that's it. These damn companies."

"It's normal, Mom. I mean, I was out for so long."

"Yes, having a baby, which is a common life event! But I guess Wall Street doesn't understand that."

"Look, I feel bad enough as it is," Wanda said, even though she wasn't overly eager to spend a chaotic holiday back home. With all that was going on, she wanted peace and quiet more than anything else.

"OK, honey, I know. All right. That's fine. There will be other times. We'll manage over here—eventually."

"Mom, listen. The first week or so is a pain, but Dad will get the hang of using crutches and will be back to his old self in no time."

Her mother was not paying attention. She had resumed her tirade, directed at no one in particular. Wanda sighed. She could listen as her mom complained, or she could cut the call short and then hear about that during their next conversation.

A knock on the door made the decision for her.

"Mom, someone's at the door. I have to get it before the knocking wakes Nelly from her nap."

Her mother definitely understood that. While she wasn't happy with Wanda's relationship (or lack thereof) with Nelly's father, she had become a doting grandmother and thought of Nelly's comfort before all else.

"Yes, yes, go ahead," she said. "Call me back later so I can speak to my sweetheart, OK?"

Wanda dropped her phone on the couch and hurried to the door. Nelly's room was far enough away that she wouldn't likely be disturbed by a gentle knock or even a doorbell, but Wanda didn't want to take any chances. She pulled open the door, expecting maybe a delivery person, and then froze.

"Wanda… I… I've come by a couple of times…"

Max. She had never seen him bundled up for winter before. Her memories had been summer and sunshine, jeans and T-shirts. And here he stood wearing a brown duffle coat, his hands stuffed in the pockets. Then he ran a hand through his hair in that nervous manner of his. She focused on these details to distract herself from the fact that Max was standing within arm's reach.

Her heart was beating a mile a minute. What to say? What to say?

"You've come by before?" she murmured.

"Can I come in?"

Wanda nodded and stepped back, nearly tripping over the collection of high heels in the vestibule.

Max tossed his coat onto a hook, and she led him into the living room that he had gotten to know well more than a year ago. Would he notice the small pile of baby toys in the corner, or would he be too disturbed by her Saturday morning look to notice anything else? With

no make-up, a ponytail and sweatpants, she was not at
her best.

"Sit down, please." Her voice sounded stiff,
unnatural, and she could kick herself for it. "So when did
you come by... um... or get back?"

"Over a month ago, I was here briefly. I came by, but
no one was around. Then I came back last week. I tried
to see you a couple of times. You must work late."

"I was on a business trip."

"How are things?"

"OK." *You should tell him about Nelly right now.* Galina's
voice echoed clearly in Wanda's head, as if she were right
there in the room coaching her.

"Are you back for the holidays?" she said instead.
Though Wanda could pull off successful presentations in
front of clients, she found herself paralyzed with fear as
she faced Max. This was going to be very, very bad. She
could feel it. And it was her own fault. How could she
have possibly made such a terrible decision?

"Longer," he said. "I've finished my mission. I just
got a job in neurology at Bichat."

"Congratulations. That's a great hospital."

"I missed you."

She looked down.

"Have you found someone else?"

She shook her head.

"I thought... because you stopped calling..."

"The connections were so bad, I could never reach
you."

"Yeah, I know," he said, with the lopsided grin that
always made her heart race. "The worst conditions for a
long-distance relationship."

"And you didn't email," she added. She hoped her
tone didn't sound too defensive or accusatory. She was
having trouble acting nonchalant.

"Network problems." He ran a hand through this

hair. "I know, it's hard to maintain a relationship that way. And I regret that."

"Do you regret that you went?"

"Sometimes." His eyes met hers, and she could read in them *because of you*. Her heart soared, but she wouldn't let herself feel the joy. He continued, "But I did some good there. I can't regret that."

"I understand. I'm glad you went." She meant it. As hard as it was, part of what she loved about Max had been this will to help those in need.

And then it began, softly, then louder. Nelly's cry, as she woke from her nap. The crying had intensified since Wanda's return from her travels. At first, Wanda thought it was teething, but the crying continued well after the gleaming white tooth poked its way through Nelly's gum. And it was then that Wanda was sure this sadness, this stress, had nothing to do with teeth.

Wanda spent every second she could with her daughter, yet guilt still gripped her heart. No matter how she managed the rest of her time, she was away from Nelly at least ten hours a day, five days a week.

Max raised an eyebrow and glanced in the direction of the bedroom, which he also knew so well.

"Are you babysitting?"

"I'll be right back."

There was no way out, no turning back. Methodically, she walked to the bedroom, took Nelly in her arms and brought her into the living room.

"She's been occupying my time since you left."

The color drained from Max's face, and Wanda braced herself. She felt numb. Nelly wasn't crying, only gazing at Max, as if curious about this person who looked so much like her.

"You're kidding me."

"As if I could."

"Why didn't you tell me, Wanda?" His voice was

hollow, empty of emotion.

"You'd counted on that mission for years. I didn't want to stop you. I told you I understood, that it was the right thing to do."

"You still could have told me! At some point, after I was there for a few months."

"I couldn't."

A tear slid onto her cheek, and she brushed it away.

"It's too late for us now," she said. "Things are what they are. I'm not expecting anything from you."

Max stood up and walked over to the window. He gazed out at the Eiffel Tower, but Wanda was sure he wasn't seeing it. Her heart was pounding with such intensity she felt as if it were echoing through the entire apartment. Yet in reality, there was simply silence. A silence that frightened Wanda. Galina had been right. Why hadn't she listened to her?

"So that's it?" Max said, turning around. She could see the anger and frustration in his eyes. "You expect me to walk out the door as if everything was right in the world? You expect me to abandon both of you? Wanda, what the hell is going on with you?"

She wanted to tell him that she had been scared, that she hadn't wanted to lose him but then lost him anyway. She wanted to tell him that her world was upside down at the moment. She wanted to tell him that she yearned for him to stay. But none of those words would come out. Instead, she reacted with ire and annoyance, redirecting the frustrations of the past months at him.

"Everything is fine," she said between clenched teeth. "If you can't understand that I only did this for you, that I didn't want to stand in the way of your—"

"Damn it, Wanda! This is a big deal!" He shook his head and turned away from her, from them. Nelly started whimpering, then went for a full-blown wail. Wanda bounced her around, but the cries only intensified.

Max turned back to Wanda, reached out a hand to touch her arm. His eyes had softened. But a voice that Wanda couldn't control spoke before she could stop it.

"Just go. We don't need you."

Max's gaze turned to ice. He brushed past them, grabbed his coat and slammed the door.

Chapter 10

Wanda wasn't sure what had become harsher: the chill in the Parisian air or the chill in her office. She and Louis hardly spoke. As a matter of fact, she hardly spoke to anyone. Most of her time was consumed by client meetings and research at her computer. She didn't have time for water cooler chitchat or drinks after hours. After hours she was doing one of three things: working, spending time with Nelly or sleeping.

But no one seemed to understand. Flora and Sam and the others—the same group she used to head to the bar with—stumbled into the office later than she ever did, then spent twenty minutes getting coffee, then took several smoke breaks, then took a long lunch, then complained about how many hours they worked as she hurried out the door to pick up Nelly.

And then there were the occasions when they stopped her as she was about to leave. Wanda knew what to expect. She was used to the comments by now. *You're no fun! Just because you've had a baby doesn't mean your social life has to end! Haven't you ever heard of a babysitter?* And the list went on.

She would shrug if she was in a decent mood or give them a dirty look if the day had been particularly difficult, but she would never explain, give in or defend herself.

Sometimes she thought she deserved it. She remembered criticizing not only Elodie for avoiding the after-work routine but also her colleague Kate. Wanda had been the one to roll her eyes when Kate, back from maternity leave, never had time for an evening drink. Now, the memory turned her face scarlet in shame.

On this mid-December day, Wanda hardly heard the rain pattering on the window just beyond her cubicle, hardly noticed the excitement or voices around her. Her attention was on the charts on her screen, and she didn't like what she was seeing. It was a bad year for the market. But that didn't matter to Wanda, and it didn't matter to her clients. In a bad year, she could still give them a decent return. She always did. But in the past, she wasn't starting from negative. In the past, she had managed her funds closely, keeping them out of the danger zone. Yet now, despite how hard she worked, fund performance had reeled out of her control. She could bring it back, but it would take time. The damage Thomas had done couldn't be corrected in a quarter.

And then, as she was about to close out a position, Thomas was standing by her side with a glass of champagne in his hand.

"Here," he said, holding it out to her.

"What's this all about? A holiday party?" Wanda knitted her brow and stood up. But she didn't take the glass. She was wary of any sort of good news coming from someone who was unable to keep a solid fund rolling for three months.

"I've been promoted to senior fund manager," he said.

What? she wanted to cry out. That was *her* level. She was a senior fund manager. And she had worked her ass off to get there. Sadly, she wasn't even given the position with this sort of pomp and circumstance. By default, as a series of managers quit almost simultaneously, the big bosses were left with the choice of Wanda, Kate (who was on an extended maternity leave), or an intern. That had happened three years ago. And today, Thomas ruined her funds, yet management promoted him to senior fund manager? Just because he was some big shot's cousin. Kate had been waiting for that kind of promotion for years.

"Congratulations," Wanda said stiffly. Then she glanced at the glass, still in midair between them. "And thanks, but I don't drink on the job."

After Thomas made his way back to the others, laughing, drinking and talking, Wanda settled into her seat and executed her trade as if nothing had happened. She pushed aside the anger and the feelings of injustice, and forced herself to focus. Louis was an ass. Thomas was an ass. And the others were being assholes too. She couldn't reason with people like that. She glanced over at Flora, who laughed and shared stories with Thomas as if they were the best of friends. Flora had spent less and less time stopping by Wanda's desk to chat. None of them understood Wanda's priorities. They thought she was being snooty and unsociable because she didn't have time for cocktails once a week.

"How about a coffee?" Maddie's voice.

Wanda turned around and smiled, relieved it wasn't Thomas with another glass of champagne or an asinine comment.

"Come on," Maddie coaxed, sensing her hesitation. "Your eyes are red. You could use a break, my dear."

Wanda yanked off her glasses and rubbed her eyes, not caring if she smudged her mascara. She was tired. Nelly hadn't been sleeping nights and neither had she. She thought of Max, that painful encounter only two days ago. Every time her phone rang, she jumped. Would it be him? It wasn't. And what would she even say? She didn't know.

"Well?" Maddie said.

"In the kitchen?" Wanda suggested meekly.

"No, let's go out. Just around the corner. It will do you some good."

❧

They sat at the far end of the counter at the café that had turned sleepy at this mid-afternoon hour. The bartender slid two coffees over to them, and Wanda took a sip.

"What do you think?" she asked, turning to Maddie.

"About Thomas and the promotion?"

"Yes."

"I think trouble is brewing."

"Yeah," Wanda said with a snort, "with him in charge of even one fund, the company will go down the toilet."

"That's where you're wrong, Wanda. They've assigned him the most competent associate fund manager. Thomas will sign off on all of her good decisions. And everything will be fine."

"That's disgusting," Wanda said. She took another sip of coffee, but it didn't melt the icy feeling inside. "Look at Kate, she's been waiting for this kind of position and deserves it."

"Kate left the company, Wanda."

"What? When did that happen?"

"When you were in China. One minute she was meeting with Louis, and the next, she was carrying a cardboard box with her belongings out the door."

"I thought she was out sick."

Maddie shook her head.

"What happened? And why didn't Louis at least tell

us?"

"No one likes talking about sexual harassment, Wanda."

"What?" A shiver ran up and down her spine. *I'm not the only one.*

Maddie lowered her voice and her gaze as she spoke. "Rumor has it she didn't appreciate Louis' advances, nor did she appreciate that he strongly suggested she get an abortion if she hoped to keep her job."

"She's pregnant?"

"Third child on the way."

"How long had this been going on? The harassment, I mean." Wanda's mind was racing. Kate was a beautiful woman with long blond hair and a dazzling smile. She turned heads inside and outside of the office. But she was also married and the mother of two—well, now almost three. The idea of Louis putting sexual pressure on her made Wanda want to gag.

"So she just left?" Wanda asked. "Quietly, like that?"

"Well, she's filed a lawsuit for harassment. And word has it there are several other women in Whilt offices around the world who've filed for harassment or discrimination, naming male employees in the suit."

Wanda thought of her own situation since she'd returned from maternity leave, but she wasn't ready to talk about it with Maddie or anyone else. She admitted it: She was still in denial. *This nightmare may be happening to these other women, but it's not happening to me. My case was isolated. One—OK two—times.*

She turned back to Maddie. "What sort of trouble were you referring to? Just this about Kate, right? Management's reaction, maybe?"

Maddie reached over and squeezed Wanda's arm.

"Wanda, you have to be prepared for any outcome." She pronounced the words slowly, deliberately. Wanda's stomach flip flopped. She dropped her cup onto the saucer with a clang. If she drank another mouthful, she would vomit. Maddie's words echoed in her head.

"This isn't about me," Wanda snapped.

"Wanda, Wanda, listen, calm down. I didn't mean to upset you. I want you to understand something."

"What?"

"Whilt does not like women with babies and toddlers."

"But you had children, and you went far in your career at Whilt! This can't happen to everyone!" *If I push it away, if I say it's not true, it won't be true.*

"Slowly but surely, things have changed, Wanda. Ironic, isn't it? You would think the work environment for women would improve as time goes by, but that isn't necessarily the case. And it depends on management too. Climates change at companies."

Wanda sat in silence. Her eyes dropped to her fingers as they played with the strap of her handbag. She wasn't one to believe what someone told her without proof to back it up, but Maddie's comments were hardly out of the blue. *They made sense.* And that couldn't mean anything positive for her future at the company.

"Are you saying I'll be next? Driven to suicide or driven out the door?"

"I don't know," Maddie said. She swallowed the last few drops of coffee and pushed her cup and saucer to the side. "But I do think you should be prepared."

"To find a new job?"

"Maybe."

৽৹৵

Wanda returned to her desk with a glumness that was impossible to hide. But it didn't matter. No one paid much attention to her. She was like a walking spreadsheet, speaking only of fund performance, annual reports and other dry subjects while the others talked about weekend trips or evenings bar hopping.

Something on her desk caught her eye as she slipped out of her coat and tossed it onto the back of her chair. A large manila envelope with her name written across the top. She opened it and froze. A preliminary performance evaluation. She scanned the words, the numbers, the cacophony on the page. None of this made sense. She hadn't been told she'd be receiving a preliminary review. And the information it contained, in many instances, was false or skewed.

Deciding to go straight to the source, she marched to Louis' office and stood in the doorway. He glanced at her, then down at his papers, then back up again.

"Sorry, I thought you were Elisabeth," he said, referring to his secretary. "What can I do for you, Wanda?"

"What's this, Louis?" she asked, waving the performance review in the air as she took a step closer. "We need to talk."

"Have a seat."

She settled into the messiness of his office and glared at him.

"We've started doing preliminary reviews, to give employees an idea of what to expect. It's to help you as you progress toward your goals." His voice was businesslike, but his eyes still undressed her.

"This review is unfair." She refused to break away from his gaze and show her discomfort.

"What do you mean by unfair?"

"You're comparing my fund performance with that of managers managing entirely different products in different regions. That wasn't how it was done in the past. And the goals—they're unattainable. You're expecting my funds to be plus five by the end of the quarter, meaning in about two weeks? The only thing happening in the market right now is window dressing! Investors buying a few high flyers to make their funds look good. You can't expect a major change in performance."

"Wanda, if you have a problem with your evaluation, you can contact human resources. As far as I'm concerned, it's fair."

"Human resources? But they don't understand what I do on a daily basis! You are the one who should do it— and who should know better."

"Or you can meet with me privately, babe. I'm sure we could work something out."

Wanda's mouth opened, but words wouldn't come out. Even with Kate's lawsuit dangling above his head, Louis wasn't changing his ways. *Because he doesn't believe Kate will win. He doesn't believe any woman would win.*

Wanda rose from her seat as Louis' eyes wandered from her eyes to her chest. She turned and walked out.

Chapter 11

"My life is so screwed up." Wanda sank deeper into Galina's couch and brought the fishbowl of a wineglass to her lips. She'd spilled her story—everything—to Galina. Well, not the part about Max. She wanted to handle that on her own, if there was anything to handle. At this point, she might never even see him again. No. She wouldn't think of that right now. She had enough troubles with all that was unfolding at Whilt. But at least she wasn't completely alone since she'd shared her anguish with her best friend. Even though the problems remained, she did feel as if some of the weight had been lifted from her shoulders.

Galina had listened patiently, with that unemotional attorney face, then asked questions, all the while refilling their wine glasses and little dishes of crackers that only she had been eating. It was girls' night. Charles was out of town on business, and Wanda and Nelly had come over to spend the night. Usually that meant watching movies, getting drunk, laughing. But tonight the drinking wasn't accompanied by movies or giggles.

The only giggles came from Anya's bedroom as she

tried to convince the babysitter to let her stay up just a little longer. Nelly was already sleeping soundly.

Galina's unemotional expression had transformed into the wheels-turning expression. She'd tucked her long, thin legs underneath her and looked like an exotic cat ready to pounce from the armchair.

"So what are you cooking up?" Wanda asked with a sigh. "There's no solution, you know. I wanted to fight, but there's no way—"

"Of course there's a way," Galina said. She stood up and paced in front of the window just as the Eiffel Tower began to twinkle. For five minutes on the hour. Midnight. "Wanda, you have to seek legal advice."

"Well, I'm asking *you*. Isn't that good enough? You *are* an attorney."

Galina rolled her eyes.

"Wanda, I'm talking to you as a friend. You need advice from an attorney whose specialty is labor law—"

"That's your specialty," Wanda interjected.

"*And* who's used to defending employees," Galina continued. "I've defended *employers*, remember?"

Wanda sighed, set down her glass and rubbed her eyes. "I'm not really motivated to do it, not now. Sure, everything looks pretty bad, but I haven't been fired or put on probation. Maybe I'm overreacting. Louis' words are just that—words."

"You're not overreacting. I can tell you that for certain—and from the point of view of an attorney who has seen companies pull the wool over employees' eyes plenty of times. They are setting you up, Wanda. They have established goals that are impossible for you to attain. Therefore, you will fail, and they will have the excuse they need to fire you. Louis is playing a role in that and harassing you to boot. It's quite a cocktail."

Wanda shivered as her friend said "fire you." Words she hadn't allowed to enter her mind were now stuck there.

"I knew something was up when you told me about that heavier workload," Galina said.

"You probably knew something was up because of the look on my face."

"That too." Galina smiled then—one of her serious, take-charge smiles—and sat down next to Wanda. "Listen, I'm going to take some notes on this, do a bit of research and then get you in touch with an attorney."

"How about you? If I end up suing the company, that is."

"I'm on sabbatical."

"I know. But how about coming out of sabbatical? I think you miss working." Wanda had noticed more than once how Galina eagerly joined in conversations about Charles' cases or spent spare time doing research.

Galina lowered her eyes, and Wanda sat up straight, surprised at catching a sliver of weakness in her friend. This was an extremely rare occurrence.

"I'm right, aren't I? If I do decide to sue the company—and I'm not sure that I will—but if I do, this would be the perfect opportunity for you to return to law."

The idea sounded overly simplistic, ridiculous even, as if cooked up by an eager teenager. Heat rose into Wanda's cheeks. She hated sounding silly. Yet the thought of Galina taking control of this unwieldy situation comforted her.

Galina quickly regained her composure, her golden eyes now steady and filled with the usual decisiveness.

"This is about you, Wanda. It's not about me. When I decide to return to work, you'll be the first to know. You're always the first to know." Her voice softened, and she squeezed Wanda's hand. "But it's not the right time. I'd promised myself to stay on sabbatical until Anya turned six. I've got two more years. And in any case, I'm not the right attorney for you."

But Wanda knew her friend was indeed the best attorney she could possibly have on her side. And that's what she communicated with the look she gave her. Still, she knew there was no convincing Galina. Her whole life, Galina had only been forced into a decision by one person—herself.

Wanda thought back to their college days. Galina had always run the show. Even in class, she managed to convince professors to change the date of a test or recognize her unconventional analysis of a situation. She had a certain charisma that came with self-assurance.

Perhaps all of this self-assurance came from her enchanted life. Galina was used to castles, champagne and elegant dresses. Her father had been a Russian diplomat. Galina didn't know which country to call home after living in Russia, France, England, the United States and her birthplace, Nigeria. She was told she was adopted, but she knew better. She had her father's eyes. Yet Galina did not waste time mulling over situations that couldn't be changed, especially when they didn't present a problem. Her parents had adored her and shielded her from hardship. And this built her into the confident woman Wanda had relied on since the day they met.

Conversely, Wanda's childhood hadn't included castles and champagne. Just a comfortable uneventful bunch of years growing up in the lower level of a two-family house in Cambridge. Cold winters skating on Frog Pond, warm summers lounging on the Common. Both of her parents were teachers at a local high school so they would take her on trips during the long summer break: New York City to visit museums, the Cape for a beach holiday, a road trip through New England. That sort of thing. Nothing exotic and international about Wanda's early days. Yet somehow, she and Galina, in spite of their vastly different experiences, easily fit together like pieces of a puzzle.

Wanda finished her wine and set her empty glass on the coffee table. "I'm sure you at least have an opinion? About how this is going to go."

"They will fire you, Wanda. Sooner or later. But I think you realize that. This company is used to doing anything to come out on top. Take what you told me about Xavier. You can't stop Whilt from doing something illegal. But you can fight for justice afterward, and justice will be served. It's essential to be proactive, to attack them before they can attack you. Because you do have reason to attack them."

Wanda suddenly felt sick. All of the wine made her stomach churn, bubbling up from within. Or maybe it was just those words she didn't want to hear. In any case, she finished the evening in the bathroom, crouched over the toilet.

Chapter 12

Christmas Eve. Wanda had ignored Hanukkah, hadn't lit a single candle in the antique Menorah that remained stuffed in a closet. She had pretty much ignored the Christmas spirit too, refusing Galina's multiple invitations to dinner and eschewing any form of decoration. She would usually decorate for both holidays. Not an ostentatious display, but the Menorah on the mantel and a waist-high Christmas tree with a mismatched assortment of bulbs on its branches. This time, though, she had been so immersed in the worries about her job and the disastrous encounter with Max that she couldn't care less about holiday décor.

So there she was, at her desk at five p.m. on Christmas Eve, when the swirl of office gossip finally reached her ears.

"You mean you didn't see today's *Times*?" one voice asked. "Check this out." The pattering of footsteps as the few left in the office at this late hour on the day before a holiday ran to hover over a computer.

"Fuck." Another voice.

"They are so screwed." Another.

Wanda sank lower into her seat and opened *The Times'* website. She'd rather get the truth straight from the source than sit around gossiping with the bunch over in the corner.

Her breath caught in her throat as she read the headline and scanned the article. Ito had been arrested for his illegal bitcoin activities. And Whilt's Asian funds had been seized. The Japanese government, investigating Whilt's involvement with Ito, considered ousting the company from the country. The article made no mention of Xavier Laval, but his name was on the tongue of every whisperer she heard over the next twenty minutes.

Louis had already jumped ship, off to Chamonix for a fireside Christmas at the family chalet. Maddie was long gone too. Only the few holiday stragglers, underlings and singles, sniffed around for clues like a pack of wild dogs. Their questions, curses and suppositions echoed in Wanda's ears, but she remained frozen at her desk. Her only thoughts were for Xavier and Rita. Were they OK? She texted Rita, knowing she was always up late, always plugged in. Then she gathered her coat and handbag, and headed out of the office before she would be forced into that frenzy of mad animals trying to find out exactly what had happened with Whilt in Japan.

"We're OK and coming home next week. Don't worry." The message from Rita lit up the phone as Wanda stood by the window watching the rain fall. She let out a sigh of relief and texted back, "Relieved. Merry Christmas to both of you in spite of all this. See you soon."

Then she scooped up Nelly and sank onto the couch. Nelly latched onto her bottle and inhaled her milk in record time. The baby's crying jag had ended, and now she rested comfortably against her mother's chest.

"Growth spurt, little one?" Wanda said with a smile. She cuddled Nelly, then chatted with her like she was a small adult. "You know, next time the holidays will be better. You'll wait for Santa, leave out a few cookies. This year, you're a little young for all of that. But you still have some presents."

With one hand, Wanda unwrapped a tiny pink silk dress from her parents—totally impractical but charming—a stack of cozy pajamas and some books from Galina and then some noisy rattles and a Chinese dress that she picked up during her trip. Nelly grasped eagerly at the paper.

The phone rang, and Wanda popped a pacifier into Nelly's mouth and settled her into the lounger with a few of the board books. Nelly quickly spit out her pacifier and began to chew on the corner of the one shaped like a giant red apple. Wanda grinned. Even when she was unhappy, Nelly could make her smile. Then she answered the phone. Galina.

"Thanks for the lovely gifts!" she said, trying to sound cheerful.

"How about coming over, Wanda? You're depressing me, you know that, right? Thinking of you and Nelly alone there."

"I'm exhausted, Galina, and better off like this. Really. You're doing me a favor."

Silence for a few seconds. Wanda was almost expecting Galina to mention the article in *The Times*. But then she remembered this would be the one day of the year, with an elegant dinner to prepare, that Galina would not be plugged in to the latest news. At least not until Charles got back from the office.

"Charles home?" Wanda asked.

"Not yet. I'm hoping by eight. You'll stop by tomorrow, right? For a casual tea in the afternoon. You promised."

"Yeah, we'll be there."

"Good. Merry Christmas, Wanda."

"A merry one to you too."

With a sigh, Wanda dialed her parents' number. They would be having dinner later at her aunt's house. A big to-do with the Catholic side of the family. Right now, Wanda's mother would be wrapping gifts, last minute as usual.

The conversation was brief, mainly because Wanda lied and said she would be heading out to a holiday party in about ten minutes. It was easier this way. Her mother wouldn't worry about her sitting home alone with a bowl of chips and a glass of wine in front of the computer screen.

So after Nelly cooed into the phone enough to delight her grandmother, Wanda hung up and declared her Christmas social duties finished.

Wanda set Nelly down in the baby lounger, bounced it with her foot and checked her Whilt email account. She had sent out a holiday greeting to all her clients and a few of them kindly replied. Thankfully, none of them had sent hate mail.

Wanda's stomach growled, and her eyes fled to the clock. It was quarter to eight, and she hadn't eaten a thing since the stale croissant for breakfast. No wonder she was starving. She glanced over at Nelly, who was nodding off, and then made her way to the kitchen with visions of leftover pizza dancing in her head.

Just as she opened the refrigerator, the doorbell rang. Galina. She had probably sent Charles here to drag them over. Wanda cringed but knew she couldn't ignore the bell. So with a reticent step, she approached the door.

Raindrops fell from Max's hair onto the doormat. Wanda's heart raced with joy and panic all at once. The person she wanted desperately to see, yet his presence—

so decisive, so steady—frightened her. From the very start, a tiny voice in her head had told her Max was *the one*, but after everything that had happened, she was scared to take the leap of faith and lose herself in a relationship. And now especially, at the worst of times. How could she focus on romance when her professional world was crumbling?

But at the moment Max was gazing into her eyes, and she had to say something, do something.

"No umbrella?" she said.

"It wasn't supposed to rain. Would have made more sense if it snowed this time of year, right?" He shrugged.

"What are you doing here?" she asked. "On Christmas Eve, I mean. Don't you have better things to do? You could have gone to your brother's."

"I was hoping to spend it with you... with both of you."

"But you were angry—"

"Can I come in?"

Wanda felt her face go hot, and she looked down, trying to hide the embarrassing blush that would only worsen.

"Yeah, sure." She stepped back to let him in.

Together, they arranged his dripping coat, scarf and shoes in the vestibule. His arm brushed against hers, sending a shiver up her spine. Their eyes met for an instant, but she turned away. Then she scolded herself for thinking, feeling and behaving like someone who was in love. *Get a grip*, she pleaded with her practical side. But she wasn't sure that practical side was listening.

When they reached the living room Wanda noticed Max was carrying two bags.

"Food," he said, lifting one. "And presents," he said, nodding at the other. "You don't think I would come over and impose."

"I might have been going out," she said, crossing her

arms, then realizing that dressed in jeans and a sweatshirt, she didn't look very convincing. At least she hadn't taken off her makeup yet, and she'd freed her hair from her staid workday ponytail. "But I'm not going out. I mean, what if I was, and you'd gone through that effort for nothing?"

"But you're not, and I didn't, right?"

She nodded. OK, she needed to regroup, just be normal. She let out a slow breath and gazed at Nelly sleeping in the lounger.

"She looks so peaceful," Max said as he bent down next to her and gently touched a tiny hand.

"She's a good sleeper. Once she's out, she's out... Um, what would you like to drink?"

"I took care of that. Check out the bags."

Wanda glanced into one bag, the fragrance of lemongrass telling her it would be one of her favorites, Thai food, and then checked out the second bag. A bottle of champagne had just started to bead with sweat as it went from the cold outdoors to the heat of the apartment. And next to it, two boxes Wanda pretended not to see.

She allowed herself to smile at Max.

"You didn't have to do all this."

"I wanted to. I'm sorry I ran out the other day. I should have realized you were under a lot of pressure."

She looked away, fleeing eye contact. His words were music to her ears, yet she wasn't ready to hear them. She didn't want to be faced with more decisions, putting her in the position to make more mistakes.

Max popped the cork and filled their glasses as Wanda opened the take-out containers and spread them out on the coffee table. They settled down on the throw pillows she had scattered on the floor.

Max touched his glass to hers.

"To fresh starts," he said.

"You're very forgiving—too forgiving." She took a sip and felt the bubbles tickle their way down her throat.

"It doesn't always have to be complicated, Wanda."

Yet somehow it was in every aspect of her life. She sighed and leaned back against the couch, her hair pooling into a silky chocolate-colored mass on the cushion. Her very best feature was that mane, and most of the time it was pulled into a strict ponytail or chignon, the most practical styles for work. Max reached out and raked his hand through her hair, and for five seconds she was tempted to make things easy. She was tempted to forget about work, forget about protecting herself from heartbreak, and throw herself into Max's arms. Emotions, after all, were what had always ruled her behavior.

And that's how I got into this mess to start with, she thought.

"I'm hungry," she announced, hoping and yet deep down inside not hoping, to break the magic.

Max smiled. "Help yourself. Here… Sorry it's not too fancy." He handed her a plastic fork, clearly remembering she was incompetent with chopsticks.

She shrugged and piled hot noodles onto her plate.

"That's OK," she said, sheepish. "I was ready to resort to cold pizza before you arrived."

They ate in silence, their eyes moving to the Eiffel Tower as the five minutes of blinking illumination began. Wanda thought of their first kiss, beneath the tower like two silly tourists. She shouldn't feel embarrassed. They lived in the neighborhood after all. This was their stomping ground. She felt her face go hot and readied herself to use the spiciness of the sauce as an excuse.

"I can't look at it without thinking of us," Max said, as if reading her mind.

Wanda closed her eyes and took a deep breath. If she didn't say something, push the subject forward, she would suffer all evening and probably longer.

"Max, you were angry—furious, actually—and you walked out. I told you we didn't need you. Why did you come back?"

"I'm sorry," he said, his eyes downcast.

"You're sorry? I was the one who should have—"

"Look, it's easy to say that after the fact. As ridiculous as it seems, I understand why you did what you did." Then he looked up. She tried to turn away, but his eyes held her gaze, their intensity unavoidable. "The one thing I don't understand is why you're pushing me away now that I'm back, now that I know."

"Because I don't want to be with someone who feels forced to be with me!" The words came out before Wanda could stop them. She bit her lip. She hadn't even realized that had been her reason, but in fact it was—in all honesty. That was the big mistake she was fearing: a personal one. She had enough professional problems on her plate. She didn't want to set herself up for more drama. But she couldn't explain all of that to Max.

"I'm not forced, Wanda. I'm here because I want to be." He took her hand, and warmth traveled through her entire body. He leaned closer, and she could feel his breath on her cheek. She lowered her head, almost allowing herself to relinquish when a cry from Nelly broke into the moment.

They both jumped, blushing, then scrambled toward the lounger. Wanda reached for Nelly, who howled until her faced turned red.

"Colic?" Max asked. He might have been startled by the first shriek, but he obviously wasn't intimidated by a crying baby.

"No, just needs some milk and a diaper change." She bounced Nelly into the bedroom, while Max said something about preparing a bottle. She told him where to find the formula, and when she returned to the room, it was ready. He held out his arms, and gingerly, Wanda passed the baby to him. Nelly sucked down the milk at the speed of light.

"Hungry girl," he said.

"Yeah, like me, and speaking of which, I'll use this free minute to wolf down the rest of my dinner." She tried her best to use this interruption as a way to get the night back on the platonic track. But Nelly wasn't on her side. In minutes, the baby was fast asleep, and Max carried her into her room.

Still, Wanda wasn't ready to dive right in as if the separation had never occurred. As soon as Max returned, she launched her plan of attack: asking him questions about his work in Africa, about his new job in Paris, about anything that kept the subject far from the heart of the matter. He asked her similar questions, but she choked out the words "nothing much is new" and was done with it.

By the time they'd reached the bottom of the champagne, she had fallen asleep on Max's shoulder.

༅

When she woke up, Max was gone. She squinted dizzily and collapsed back into the pillows. What time was it anyway? She rolled over and gazed at the clock: eleven a.m. In a panic, she stumbled over the sheets and across the hall to Nelly's bedroom—where the baby slept peacefully in her crib. A note was taped to the edge. Wanda tore it off and quickly scanned it.

Wanda,

I spent the night on the couch and got up a few times for Nelly. You looked so exhausted… I thought you deserved a good night's rest. I have lots of sleepless nights to make up to you, so I figured

I'd better start now. Sorry I had to leave, but I'm working Christmas Day.

Max

Wanda shivered with delight, then stopped. She wasn't about to fall for him like a giddy teenager, now was she? *Have some self-control,* she ordered herself. It only got worse when she walked into the living room and saw the unopened gifts. She must have passed out before she even had a chance to pull them out of the bag. Like a thief fearing discovery, she ripped open the box with Nelly's name on it. Inside, a soft, cuddly stuffed bear with the little girl's name inscribed on one foot. Quickly, she moved to the second one. With shaking fingers, she pulled out a wooden handcrafted necklace, "from Africa" inscribed on a little tag. He'd remembered her passion for necklaces. She smiled, then returned to her state of panic.

She had to diffuse the situation, bring a sense of calm back to her tumultuous life. She grabbed her cell phone and scrolled down to his number. She still had it, of course.

Wanda sent him a polite text message to thank him for the gifts and the lovely evening. Polite and nothing more.

"Merry Christmas, Wanda," was his reply.

Chapter 13

Whilt wasn't kicked out of Japan, but Xavier was—sent away by the company with orders never to return. Rita quit out of solidarity and returned to Paris with Xavier.

It was two days after Christmas, and Wanda sat across from Rita at a café around the corner from the office. She looked tired, with bags under her eyes that Wanda had never noticed before. Her usual spunkiness remained, but it was tempered by the worries of the past weeks. Rita had sought Wanda out, calling her and saying they had to meet as soon as possible.

"I have to warn you," Rita said as the waiter set two cups of coffee on the table. "There is illegal money in the other fund too, the one that wasn't shut down."

"Why should I care?" Wanda asked.

"They plan to consolidate it with the new fund you'll be managing. They'll say you verified the investors and investments, even though you haven't. And if you do check out the fund and say you want to kick out the illegal money, they'll fire you. Believe me, Wanda."

And Wanda did believe Rita, even though she

exclaimed, "What?" as if she was astonished. Just instinct in this sort of situation. Panic seized her. They could fire her at any moment. As soon as Whilt management liked, they could accuse her of investing with illegal money. They would blame Xavier for handing her the tainted fund and her for continuing it.

She'd witnessed this backwards behavior before, and at that point, she should have started worrying about her future at the company. But dumbly, she had shaken her naïve head. It happened about two years earlier. A fund manager was fired for insider trading when in fact his managers had pressured him to obtain certain reports illegally.

Wanda shivered. If she didn't have rent to pay and a baby to feed, she would have walked right then and there as Rita warned her about the latest happenings. But she didn't have that kind of freedom.

The stories of the past months—years, even—flooded her mind as she took a sip of her coffee-turned-cold. Her own situation, of course, and many others. Elodie's fall and altered performance review, Thomas' preferential treatment, Xavier's dismissal. And straight from the snake pit: Raymond Grant hijacking her hotel room and Jim Tuxford warbling *Singing in the Rain* in the office's potted plants.

Wanda brought the cup to her lips, wetting her throat enough to speak.

"The place is a creepshow," she hissed.

"A creepshow?" Rita wrinkled her brow and smirked.

"The way Whilt treats employees, treats people—"

"No explanation required," Rita said, holding up her hand. "Your deduction seems quite sound."

"What will you and Xavier do?" Wanda asked. "Will you stay in Paris, even with the job market as it is?"

Rita looked down at the table a bit uncomfortably. Wanda raised an eyebrow. Her question hadn't been particularly personal. Wanda wasn't one to pry, and now she squirmed, as if she had been intrusive.

"This can't go beyond the two of us, but Xavier and I settled with the company. Xavier had more dirt to spill, and Whilt knew he would do it. So they settled. It's not like we've become millionaires—far from it—but at least we don't have to rush right out and find jobs. It gives us some breathing room. But I shouldn't be telling anyone. We've agreed not to speak about it."

"No worries about me telling anyone," Wanda said. "I'm not exactly a social butterfly at Whilt these days."

ঙ৽ৄ৶

"You have the right to refuse the Asia funds," Galina said over the wire-rimmed glasses she only wore when working. Wanda hadn't seen them in ages. Galina was poring over her friend's employment contract and taking notes. Wanda had arrived in a disheveled whirlwind, baby in one arm and briefcase in the other, right after work. Three glasses of wine and a sleeping baby later, Wanda had filled Galina in on the latest developments.

Now, her breath caught in her throat.

"I have the right to say 'no' to Whilt about something?" she finally choked out.

"You most certainly do." Galina's voice was all business. "Read this line." She thrust the paper into Wanda's face and at the same time broke it into vernacular. "You were specifically hired as a manager of European funds. That means, if they want to expand your role, they have to offer you a new contract, and you have the right to accept or decline. There are many other points in this contract I don't like. No, I don't like them at all." She shook her head and scribbled notes onto her legal pad.

"So what does this mean? What should I do?"

Galina removed her glasses, set them on the coffee table that separated the two women, and looked Wanda straight in the eye with the powerful gaze that meant she was calling the shots.

"It means you have to refuse this new assignment, citing the fact that it is not in your contract. French labor laws are strict. And if Whilt can't respect them, well, maybe Whilt shouldn't be operating on French soil."

Wanda felt her stomach sink. Sure, she'd managed to speak her mind to Louis on a few occasions, or tell off nobodies like Thomas. But the idea of going straight to the top and rebelling—even if she was right—terrified her. Her mouth went dry, but she tried to spit out a few words.

"Look, maybe it's not as bad as it seems. I could start out managing and then see how it—"

"Wanda! Do you realize what you're saying? Isn't what happened to Xavier enough?"

"I know, Galina. I just want to turn back the clock to the way things were before." Wanda pressed her hands against her face, blocking the world from view. She hated herself for this weakness, hated the pathetic sound of her voice. She was glad Galina was the only witness.

"But you can't," Galina said. Wanda wasn't offended by the firmness in her friend's voice and the lack of sympathy. They both knew Wanda needed this to set a fire under her, to incite her to action. "These are the cards you were dealt, Wanda. It's your turn to make a move. And you can't turn back."

Chapter 14

Wanda spent twelve hours thinking about Max's text message. *Let's go to Normandy this weekend, the three of us.* But this weekend was New Year's, and a New Year's date had implications. An Italian friend of hers once told her, "The way you spend New Year's Eve sets the tone for the rest of your year." Wanda had pooh-poohed the idea, but somehow, it always turned out to be true. So did she want to spend New Year's alone with Nelly in their apartment, at Galina's annual party with a bunch of drunk associates stumbling around or with Max at his family's house in Normandy? The answer was easy, but if she were to follow her behavior of late, she would not choose the happiest option. She would choose staying home and feeling sorry for herself.

She probably would have answered that way if it hadn't been for the conversations with Galina and Rita. They'd propelled her out of her state of indecision, of victimization.

Her choice, therefore, was Max and Normandy.

Max showed up at her door right on time, but Wanda, flustered by a personal rather than professional outing, was running late.

"Sorry, I'm just finishing up," she said as he kissed her on both cheeks. That familiar scent of *savon de Marseille* and something lemony.

"The necklace looks beautiful on you."

She blushed and touched her neck, feeling the smooth wood against her skin.

"It's a beautiful gift."

They gathered up the mounds of baggage in the hallway. "It's Nelly, not me," Wanda said. "Can't travel light any more." She remembered when they last went to Normandy, with only one backpack for both of them.

"That's OK, the trunk is big enough," Max said with a grin that made her heart race.

He'd rented a car, fully equipped with baby gear, and off they went under a sky that spelled snow.

"We just have to get there before it starts," he said as they sped along the highway.

They talked about lighthearted, impersonal subjects the whole trip. She'd forgotten how easy it was to talk with Max, how he carried her thoughts so far from the office and work. No one else had ever been able to do that. Since her earliest days in the working world—at her only employer, Whilt—Wanda's conversations often had revolved around her job or some related subject, such as the stock market or the economy. It was her comfort zone.

But somehow, right away, Max had coaxed her out of it and into the world of normalcy. She could talk about paintings they'd seen at museums, or a soccer match they'd watched on TV, silly movies, food and wine, and the strangest fashion victims parading around on certain Parisian streets. The real Wanda—before only visible to Galina—had bared herself to Max.

Two hours of small talk later, they'd passed the seaside village nearest to Max's family's house and headed up an incline facing the English Channel.

The house had been built more than a hundred years ago, and in spite of windows that let in a draft, the unevenness of the hardwood floors, and the peeling paint, it maintained a sense of charm and comfort. There was one main room downstairs, heated only by a fireplace, three bedrooms on the next floor and a bathroom under the rafters on the top floor.

Max's parents owned the house, but Max and his brother used it more often than they ever did. Wanda had never met the family. Max's parents lived in a rural area in central France, and his brother and family lived in the south. They hadn't made it to Paris or Normandy at any point during Wanda and Max's short time together.

Wanda had been to the Normandy house twice before, two weekends in a row. On a rainy day, she loved to lie in the clawfoot tub and watch droplets of water land on the skylight, but on this particular occasion it would be snowflakes, which had started to fall the minute they walked up the driveway.

Nelly got the first bath, and Wanda got the second, while Max tended to the fireplace.

She poured in a scoop of relaxing, lavender bath salts—the treat she remembered to bring for herself—and sank into the warm water until it reached her chin. The wallpaper, with its little rosebuds on a cream-colored background, was old-fashioned and peeling. Her eyes wandered over it until they reached the skylight above her head. And there the snowflakes danced, at first melting on contact with the glass, then sticking, forming a glistening carpet. Thoughts of Whilt tried to force their way into Wanda's mind, but she pushed them away. That place had taken over so much of her life. Didn't she deserve a few hours of freedom? She switched to a jazz station on the small radio just within reach and allowed the music to transport her.

By the time Wanda slipped into her terrycloth robe, multiple layers of white powder covered the skylight. She could hear Nelly squealing downstairs and Max laughing as she dressed. An unfamiliar room with a window opening to an unfamiliar view of the snow-covered lawn. Max would be staying in the room they had previously shared, with the large soft bed and a window overlooking the beach. He offered this room to Wanda, but she preferred as few memories of the past as possible.

She looked at her reflection. It was New Year's Eve, and she was here in this charming place with Max. Her heart fluttered at the thought. She couldn't waltz downstairs in a sweat suit. But she couldn't see herself putting on a sequined gown and party hat. She didn't exactly have a choice in the matter as she looked at the contents of her bag. She had hastily packed one "dressy" outfit, and now as she looked at it, she realized it would be perfect for the occasion: a short, simple gray cashmere dress. As Wanda dabbed on a bit of lip gloss, she listened to the happiness unfolding a flight below. And for a very long moment, she regretted she wasn't part of it.

ॐ

The fire had done the trick, turning the nasty chill into a warm toasty temperature that could lull anyone to sleep. It did so with Nelly, who after an early dinner and a small stack of stories was soon snoozing in Wanda's arms. The shower upstairs switched on, then off, and minutes later, Max was next to her on the couch. Casual and sexy in an oxford shirt and jeans.

"She's out," Wanda said, nodding at Nelly. Tiptoeing up the stairs in tandem, Max and Wanda set her down in the crib Max's brother had set up for the family's children. Wanda switched on the classical music station and the baby monitor, and watched as Nelly grimaced, wiggled and then settled into perfect slumber. Wanda smiled the wide smile that these days only came naturally when she looked at her daughter. Max caught her eye and took her hand. She didn't pull away, only followed him downstairs to the open kitchen where he began reheating the stack of gourmet dishes he had bought at the shop down the street from his apartment. Neither of them were cooks by any stretch of the imagination so this was as fancy as they got.

They continued with the superficial conversation typical of a new friendship until their second bottle of champagne. By then, they had taken their drinks to the fireside, and Wanda allowed her eyes to meet his, allowed the depths of her feelings to seep out.

"I've missed you," he whispered, leaning closer, his lips brushing her ear. She could have pushed him away, and it would have been over. But this was one battle she didn't want to keep fighting. One battle that now, all of a sudden, seemed unnecessary. His mouth met hers, awkwardly at first, as if afraid she might change her mind. She smiled sheepishly, and so did he, their teeth bumping. "Let's try that again," he murmured. She brought her lips to his, ran her hands down his back, untucking his shirt, feeling his skin. Her heart pounded double time. The moment she had secretly dreamed of since he had left was unfolding. His scent of soap and champagne soaked into her as they sank into the couch, peeling off layers of unwanted clothing along the way.

Wanda ended up in Max's bed, the one they had shared more than a year ago. She woke up with his arms around her, his lips against her ear. Her eyes flew open as the memory of the night before flashed through her mind. She, Wanda Julienne, had actually spent a full evening as a human being focused on her personal life rather than as a Whilt robot obeying commands and fearing fate. As she realized this, the problems of the past weeks washed over her again.

"You OK?" Max asked.

"Why?"

"You stiffened up just now. Are you regretting—"

"No." She turned to face him and melted once again as her eyes met his. "I'm tired of regretting things."

"That's good, because you're probably going to be stuck in close quarters with me today."

She knitted her brow.

"Look out the window," he continued. "We're snowed in."

Chapter 15

Wanda shouldn't have taken the call. She knew that. Wasn't seeing Louis' name flashing across the screen enough of a warning that if she were to answer, she would ruin her weekend? Yet somehow, as if under a spell, her finger swiped the screen, and Louis' voice echoed in her ear.

"Wanda, I know you're off tomorrow, but I need you back early. Raymond is passing through last minute, and you have to be here for a meeting about the Asian funds."

Wanda pulled Max's oxford shirt more tightly around herself and paced in front of the blazing fire. Goose bumps rose on her skin, from the fire and from the words she was about to say.

"Louis, I can't." Her voice tightened in her throat. "I'm snowed in, but beyond that, I'm traveling with… with a friend." She felt her face go scarlet as she said the words. Max's eyes were on her, then he turned away and carried a squirming Nelly to the window to gaze out at the snow.

"Take a damn train, Wanda," Louis said. "You have

responsibilities here. Who you're fucking comes last."

The Wanda Julienne of several months ago would have been shocked, but nothing had that effect on her today. Louis was looking for any opportunity to make her life miserable, to force her to her knees. Months ago, she might have been frightened. She might have searched for any form of transportation to take her back to Paris. She wouldn't have cared if her private life was put on the back burner, as long as whatever crisis Whilt was undergoing was solved. But now, as Wanda sat toasting in front of the fire, she knew that loyalty wouldn't pay off. And she wasn't going to use Tricia as a role model and sleep her way out of trouble.

"This is my vacation time, Louis, and my personal life comes first." Her voice didn't betray the trembling inside. "Next time, Raymond will have to plan ahead."

"No one defies Raymond Grant."

"Well, let me be the first."

Silence. Except for cries from Nelly, wailing at the top of her lungs.

"Listen, I have to go, Louis. The baby is crying. I'll see you in two days."

Wanda hung up before he could start another tirade meant to change her mind.

"What was that all about?" Max asked as he transferred Nelly into Wanda's arms.

"Nothing," Wanda said, settling down on the massive oak bench at the dining table. She ran a distracted hand through her hair, half untangling the web Max had created, and bounced Nelly on her knee.

Max set two cups of coffee on the table, and a brioche, sliced in four.

"You thought ahead," she said, trying to sound nonchalant. She took a slice of brioche and started chewing, savoring the buttery flavor. But Max wouldn't be distracted.

"Tell me, Wanda." His voice was gentle as he touched her arm. She wanted him to pull her closer, to talk about last night rather than the mess at Whilt. Her eyes met his, almost pleading to change the subject, but he wouldn't budge. She sighed.

"OK, look, Whilt has become more and more difficult—on everyone. But since I got back from maternity leave, things have taken a dive." And then she spilled the story, not meaning to go so far, but Max's kind eyes drew it from her.

"You have to leave, Wanda," he said after she finished, allowing herself finally to take a sip of coffee. "You can't put up with that harassment!"

"I can't leave. Not right now." She settled a calmed Nelly into the lounger with her rattles and turned back to him. "I have to support Nelly and myself. I have rent to pay, food to buy—"

"You can move in with me."

"No, I'm not going to rely on—" And then she stopped, realizing what he had said. Her face went hot, and she looked down, hoping he didn't notice the deep shade of red coloring neck to forehead.

"I mean it," he insisted, gathering her hands in his.

"It's too sudden. I need more time, and so do you. I can't move in with you because I can't afford not to! That's the wrong reason."

"That isn't my reason." His words were soft, coaxing, causing a ripple of pleasure to run up her spine.

It wouldn't have been Wanda's reason either, but she couldn't allow such a major change, such a distraction, to arise at this critical time in her professional life. *You're still a damn fool, putting work before anything else,* she thought. But she couldn't fight that serious voice inside, saying, *There's a time for everything, and now is the time to handle Whilt.*

Wanda sighed and shook her head.

"Max, I won't rush things." She aimed for assertive

but wasn't sure if it came out that way.

She could see the disappointment in his eyes. "I have to take care of this my way, OK?" she continued, almost as if she were apologizing.

"Wanda, this is serious. You can't ignore it."

"I won't, but I will take care of this myself, Max. I can handle it."

Max closed his eyes and pressed his hands to his temples. "I know you can, Wanda. I just... I don't want you to go through this alone."

"It will be OK," she said with a confidence she didn't feel.

"So what are you going to do?" He tore off a bit of brioche and popped it in his mouth.

She shrugged. "Galina recommends refusing the Asian funds. I have the right to, according to my contract."

"I would follow her advice if I were in your situation."

"Because she's a lawyer?"

"Because she's a lawyer *and* your friend. That's a pretty good combination."

Max and Galina met on several occasions a year ago, when the two couples went out for dinner or for a drink. Those nights out had never happened with Wanda's previous boyfriends. They had fallen into two categories: those who disliked Galina for her strong personality, and those who fantasized about sleeping with her. In both cases, it meant an evening out with Galina and her husband was impossible. Max fell into neither category. He seemed to genuinely like Wanda's best friend and the role she played in Wanda's life.

"I'll see what happens when I go back to the office," Wanda said. This time her voice was firm, and Max immediately nodded and brought his lips to her ear.

"OK," he said. "I understand. I don't want this to

ruin our weekend together. Let's forget about Whilt for now." His mouth settled on her ear, and she reached out to pull him closer. She was happy to push Whilt far from her mind. She wanted to forget about that place for a few more hours and prolong the feelings Max had stirred within.

Chapter 16

All thoughts of the holiday weekend evaporated as the heavy doors of Whilt Investment Services shut behind Wanda. The new year had started as she expected: with her fund performance in the toilet and Louis pouting as he passed her in the hall. Wanda spent the morning slouched behind her computer, executing trades, fielding calls and poring over financial reports. The tasks were the same as they had always been, but the atmosphere was so much different from years earlier. The feeling was tense, claustrophobic.

Wanda thought back to Galina's advice. She knew she had to refuse the new funds, but would she have the strength to do so? For days, she had been avoiding the whole subject. Even now, as she sat in front of her spreadsheets, she reassured herself by saying the decision hadn't yet been made. First, she wanted to find out what was happening to Xavier's funds.

She glanced around the office at the heads diligently bent in front of computer screens. She knew better than to assume they were all busily working. She'd glimpsed plenty of Facebook screens that would quickly be minimized if Louis entered the room. She could ask any of these people about the funds in question, and months earlier, she probably would have. But Wanda's trust in most of her colleagues was waning. They seemed happiest hiding from the problems, turning a blind eye or even criticizing their own colleagues if it could save their asses.

She would talk with Maddie. Decisively, Wanda rose from her seat and made her way upstairs to the small corner office.

Maddie swiveled around, a smile on her face.

"Happy New Year, dear!" She walked around the massive wood desk and kissed Wanda on both cheeks. "Holiday went well?"

Wanda nodded.

"There is a disconnect between your face and your answer," Maddie said, wincing. "Have a seat."

Maddie closed the glass door, and Wanda sighed, slowly releasing the tension that had built up in her body in the brief walk from her office to Maddie's. Walking down those halls was enough to put her on edge.

"Tell me." Maddie's voice was kind and calm, as usual.

"I was wondering about Xavier's... replacement. That was the part of the story I missed." She felt her face going hot, as if she had asked a question she didn't have the right to ask, but she willed herself to end that weak behavior. If she couldn't show strength in front of an ally, how would she possibly show it in front of the stars of the Creepshow? The thought almost made her smile.

"Tricia Warren will be managing the emerging markets and appointing some local managers to take over those funds," Maddie said, rolling her eyes. "It's part of her promotion. You remember her, don't you?"

Wanda hesitated, her voice sticking in her throat. So Tricia was at it again, working her way up the corporate ladder.

"I saw her when I was in New York but didn't realize she was in line for a promotion," Wanda said.

"It's only natural. Word has it she's pregnant, and Jeffrey Williams is the father."

Wanda's heart skipped a beat. Jeffrey was Raymond's right hand man. That's how Tricia knew about Raymond's escapades—and everything else going on in those management offices, most likely. So Tricia's plans to sleep her way to the top had worked, and more quickly than planned. Now, she was on the other side. No longer would Wanda trust her, spend the night at her apartment on a New York trip. It was one thing to fool around with those at Louis' level, and another thing to be pregnant with a company executive's child. Wanda shivered at the thought. Tricia had truly sold out. And at this point, maybe Whilt couldn't trust her either—but that was Whilt's problem, not hers.

"You look shocked. You shouldn't be. It's par for the course."

"No... I'm... I didn't know she was pregnant."

"She's only about four months along."

"I guess their treatment of Tricia will prove they don't discriminate against women who've come back from maternity leave," Wanda snapped.

"We'll see when she returns from leave."

"What does this mean for the other Asian funds?" Wanda asked. She pushed away thoughts of Tricia. Maddie was right; this was practically normal business at Whilt. Her main concern had to be the tainted funds.

"As far as I know, you'll be inheriting those if you agree to it."

"And if I don't?"

"Whilt doesn't like rebellion. But I think you know that."

They were both silent for a minute. Wanda, to her

own surprise, remained calm. She had expected that answer after all. Now the question was: Would she accept the situation or not?

She stood up and thanked Maddie, but Maddie shook her head.

"There's no reason to thank me, Wanda. I simply confirmed the bad news you probably had anticipated."

"You think I should quit, don't you?" Wanda thought back to those earlier warnings and their conversation about the company's attitude toward women with babies.

Maddie reached for Wanda's hand and squeezed it.

"No. I think you should fight."

Chapter 17

The evening would be lighthearted. Wanda promised herself that as she hiked up the five flights to Max's apartment under the stars. Beneath the rafters in Montmartre, overlooking the charming city she ignored most of the time. She had felt shameful dropping a squirming Nelly off at Galina's.

"Is this terrible parenting?" she had asked.

"Don't be ridiculous!" Galina had waved her away like a bothersome fly. "Go have fun for once. Honestly, the past few months have been so much about work that you're becoming a boring date, my friend. You and Max need time alone to build your relationship. Now go on!"

Galina's words had managed to get a smile out of her even though that had become a rather rare expression for her these days. Then she'd smiled again when Anya ran into the room and threw her arms around Nelly. The baby's eyes immediately lit up, and Wanda knew that all was well.

Max kissed Wanda tentatively as if unsure whether she would turn and run back down the stairs or continue what they had started in Normandy. She leaned into him.

She would continue what they had started.

Max ushered her into the loft with slanted skylights on each side offering a view of the city from two angles. Wanda imagined accepting Max's invitation and moving her and Nelly into this small space. Then she blushed as if he could read her mind. But Max was too busy hanging up her coat and handbag to notice her discomfort.

Keep the conversation casual if you don't want this evening to turn into a Whilt-fest, Wanda told herself.

"How was your day?" he asked.

"Quiet. I kept to myself."

Max nodded and opened a bunch of takeout boxes on the coffee table. Just because sushi was cold didn't mean it couldn't be a wintery comfort food.

"Did your boss give you any problems? After all that you told me, I worried—"

"It's OK, really," she interrupted. "Things will work out. They always have. He didn't even speak to me, so there isn't much harassment in that." But her words were empty, used only to avoid a conversation about Whilt.

She sat on the couch, her eyes on her black wraparound skirt as Max handed her a plate and fork. Her thoughts wandered back to the conversation with Maddie, but she stopped and scolded herself. How could she be thinking about work when this man she had fallen for like a ton of bricks was sitting right next to her? What was wrong with her?

Wanda chewed on a salmon roll and tried to bring herself back to some form of normal.

"How are things going at the hospital?" she asked. He hadn't told her much of anything about his new job.

"Intense—exactly the sort of work I was looking for."

"The rush of emergency care? I guess you don't go from an exciting medical trip to treating the sniffles in a neighborhood doctor's office."

He grinned.

"There are different challenges, I suppose. Right from the start, though, I was interested in hospital work."

"Any more missions on the horizon?" Wanda regretted the words as they slipped out of her mouth. There, he now knew just how interested she was in having him around.

A serious expression replaced the grin.

"No, there were so many complications over there—on various levels. It's time for me to start anew here."

His words, as simple as they were, troubled her. Had he become involved with someone over there? Had he so quickly replaced her, even for a short while? She yearned to ask the question, yet didn't want to know the answer.

His hand suddenly found hers, and their fingers entwined. She felt his warmth, saw it in his eyes. She told herself she was being paranoid and ridiculous.

"Let's not talk about work," he said. "After twelve hours at the hospital, I don't like bringing it home with me."

"Do I talk about work too much? I'm sure I must."

"Well if you do, it's not with me." His eyes sparkled mischievously.

"I'm trying to break the habit. That place is like a two-pack-a-day addiction."

"It makes you feel that good?"

"Do two packs a day really make your body feel good?" she asked.

"Well said, Doctor." He laughed so that the dimple in his right cheek appeared. The dimple she saw every day when she looked at Nelly.

⚭

Max was gone by six a.m., off for another long shift. In her half-asleep state, she remembered his lips grazing hers, his hands running through her hair as he slipped into the darkness. Now she was under the shower, alone with memories of him and their night together. But they would quickly be interrupted by Whilt. Somehow or other, any train of thought led to that destination. And she was tired of it, tired of fearing the next arbitrary decision, the next unfair judgment.

She towel-dried her hair and looked at herself in the steamy mirror. The dark circles under her eyes weren't from last night, a passionate night that had lasted nearly until morning. The only trace of that was the glow in her cheeks. No, those circles had become permanent—Whilt-induced fatigue.

As she dabbed on concealer to hide the worry marks, as she practiced the indifferent look she would wear on her face, she made her decision. It wasn't the echo of Maddie's words or Galina's that convinced her. It was the realization that whatever she did would be wrong in the eyes of Whilt managers. So she might as well do what she pleased.

Chapter 18

It was four o'clock by the time Louis agreed to speak with Wanda. In the meantime, she had settled down to admire the trend she'd first noticed a few days earlier: Her funds were recovering. Truly recovering. The strategy she'd hastily put in place several weeks ago was starting to bear fruit. She smiled in spite of the conversation she knew was awaiting her in Louis' office.

"What's going on?" Louis asked now as she sat across from him. He leaned on his desk, one eye on the cell phone that lit up with new messages every few seconds.

"Well, first, I thought I would let you know that my work is paying off. The funds are recovering. Ilcap Prestige is up three percent, and the others are up one."

"We'll need more than that to please our investors—"

"Louis, you said the funds had to be in positive territory by the end of the quarter. I told you that was impossible, yet I managed to bring the funds back a week into the new quarter. You do realize Thomas had decimated the performance of these funds, don't you? It's not a problem anyone could fix overnight."

"There are certain problems that can be easily fixed overnight, Wanda, but you refused that option." He smiled wickedly and covered her hand with his. "It's never too late, you know."

"I can't believe you said that." She pulled her hand away with disgust. Wanda regretted wearing the green V-neck sweater that dipped a little low as Louis' eyes followed the stitching.

Louis sighed and looked up at her once again. "Is that pitiful fund improvement what you wanted to see me about, Wanda? It could have waited."

Wanda took in a deep breath. She would remain calm. She had to remain calm. Management had set an impossible goal, and now that she had pretty much fulfilled it, Louis was calling it *pitiful?* Her thoughts earlier that day had been right on the mark: Whatever she did wouldn't be good enough. *Because they are looking for any excuse to force me out!*

"No, there's more. I've decided not to take on the Asian funds." Her voice didn't waver, didn't crack. A strange sense of confidence swelled within. No matter what Louis' reaction, she had done the right thing.

Louis' face went blank. Then after a few seconds, he wrinkled his brow.

"What do you mean 'you decided'? You can't decide—"

"I can decide. According to my contract, I was hired to manage European funds only. If you want that to change, you have to change my contract, and I have to agree. And I'll tell you right now: I won't agree."

"I'll have to discuss this with upper management."

Wanda stared at him through narrowed eyes. He hadn't argued or begged or criticized. He hadn't mentioned that it was such a shame she had done so much research in China only to abandon the project. He hadn't asked why she had made this decision. As soon as she had mentioned the word "contract," as a matter of fact, his cheeks had turned red. Wanda had a feeling she would no longer be dealing much with powerless Louis. Instead, she would be dealing with those who directed his every move.

∽∾

"It's time to celebrate!" Galina said as she wrapped her arms around Wanda. "Should I open champagne?"

"Because I stood up to the Creeps?"

"The Creeps?"

"Whilt management."

"That's fitting." Galina started to get up, but Wanda stopped her.

"No. No champagne. No celebration."

"I don't mean to be flippant, Wanda. I'm simply overjoyed that you're taking a stand, that you aren't letting that company intimidate you, that you aren't letting that asshole harass you."

"Thanks." Wanda shrugged. "Now what?"

"Now I want you to see Daniel Lambert, an excellent labor attorney who has successfully represented many employees against their employers."

"I'm not suing anyone, Galina."

"This isn't about a lawsuit, at least not yet. But you have to be prepared."

Wanda shook her head and got up, pacing in front of the bay window. She ignored the beauty of the Eiffel Tower, sparkling in the darkness beyond.

"Why do you always treat everything like a possible case?"

"Because everything *is* a possible case." Galina grinned and rose to meet Wanda in the center of the room. They faced each other in a friendly standoff.

"OK, you win," Wanda said, sighing. "I'll follow your

advice. I'll take this guy's number and add meeting with him to my to-do list. But if this ever reaches lawsuit stage, I want you involved, Galina. Sabbatical or not."

"We'll figure it out."

Just then, Nelly began to cry. Wanda scooped her out of the baby lounger and cuddled her against her chest, but the tears continued.

"I shouldn't have left her overnight," she mumbled half to herself.

"Don't blame yourself, Wanda," Galina said, rubbing Nelly's soft curls with one hand. "She will get used to your work schedule, you know."

"But that wasn't my work schedule, it was—"

"It was having a life," Galina said, her voice firm. "You have a right to some adult time."

"You say that, but you're staying home with Anya."

"We've had this conversation before." Galina sighed. "I have the opportunity to stay home, and it's great, but who says it's the best way? There are pros and cons in each situation—and for everyone involved."

Her eyes looked faraway, the expression that took over whenever they spoke of the sabbatical. *So who is doing the right thing and for whom?* Wanda thought. *Galina staying at home for her daughter, or me, with my all-consuming job?* There wasn't one answer. There wasn't an answer that would make everyone happy all of the time.

"I just feel like I'm doing everything wrong sometimes," Wanda murmured into the baby's neck.

Galina folded them both into her arms.

"You're not. You did the right thing at work, and you're doing the right thing as a mother too."

Chapter 19

They climbed the five flights to Rich and Deb's apartment, to the party much like the one that signaled the start of their reunion a few months ago. The pulse of music, the scent of cigarettes and the buzz of voices greeted them. The front door was open, with revelers spilling into the hallway as usual.

Wanda slipped out of her coat, revealing a shimmery short black dress and silver beads that fell to her waist.

"You look amazing," Max whispered in her ear as he tossed their coats on a chair serving as an overloaded coatrack.

Wanda smiled, another genuine smile. Despite her troubles at Whilt, at least Nelly, Galina and Max had been able to make her smile. But she didn't want to think of Whilt now.

She squeezed Max's hand and led him over to a corner where Galina and Charles were speaking with a bunch of friends from the firm. Introductions were made, pleasantries exchanged, and then the lively conversation about one of Charles' cases continued. Wanda settled into Max's arms, against a soft cushion, and both of them sipped glasses of wine that Deb had brought by.

Galina was immersed in the discussion, and commented with such passion and knowledge that Wanda and the others remained glued to the spot, as if they could listen to her all evening. Her eyes sparkled, her whole being came alive.

"No wonder she hardly ever lost a case," Max said.

Wanda nodded, but her thoughts were one step ahead, to her friend's future. How could Galina wait a couple of more years to return to law when it brought her such joy? And why couldn't she admit that she regretted the decision to stay home? The perfect Galina had the right to make a mistake or change her mind. Wanda had told her that in the past, on less important issues, and Galina had always laughed. But this was different. Wanda had sensed her friend was dissatisfied with witnessing life at the firm rather than experiencing it. And over the past four years, the situation had deteriorated. Except for occasions when Galina could put her analytical mind to work, she seemed as wilted as an old flower. This realization washed over Wanda. It hadn't been in her imagination.

Galina had been fighting this since she left the firm, and Wanda had been so absorbed in her own problems she hadn't realized the depth of her friend's distress.

Of course, Wanda could say she tried to address the problem; she tried to coax Galina to take on her case. But that wasn't really sitting down with her friend and having a heart-to-heart conversation about how happy (or not) she was with her life. *That's what we need to do,* Wanda thought. In the coming days, she would do it. Galina didn't have a monopoly on problem solving.

Wanda lifted her wine glass to her lips just as a pair of black high heels stopped in front of her. Her eyes traveled up the long legs to the clingy blue dress, the matching blue eyes and the long blond hair.

"Max, I'm surprised to see you got over us so soon." Max and Wanda stood up, a simultaneous motion as if they were one, and then stepped apart, letting this woman a step closer. Eyes turned in their direction.

"Justine, I don't think this is the right place—"

"The right place to say you lied when you said you weren't ready for commitment? You seem to be committing just fine to this woman."

She shot a patronizing smile in Wanda's direction. But Wanda, who couldn't take one more betrayal, didn't hang around to hear the rest. She moved forward blindly, only stopping to pull her coat off the top of the pile near the door. She ran down the stairs, then hailed a cab in record time. She wasn't sure if she heard footsteps or voices behind her. She had blocked out the world.

Chapter 20

Where are you?

The message from Max lit up her cell phone at one a.m. as she burrowed deeper under the dense comforter at Galina and Charles' apartment. She'd swung by their place to pick up Nelly from the nanny who'd been watching her and Anya, but instead she decided to stay. She felt safer there. She borrowed one of Galina's nightshirts and moved into the guest room—at least for the night.

The next message: *I'm at your door, and you're not here. I'm worried. I'm sorry. It's not as bad as it seems.*

Wanda snorted and switched off her phone. She blew her nose into another tissue and added it to the stack she'd started on the nightstand.

A gentle knock at the door. Galina, of course, who had followed in the next available taxi and was now kneeling at the bedside, pressing her cheek against Wanda's forehead. Wanda's tears returned in full force, stirred up by Galina's sympathy.

"That's OK, cry it out," she instructed as she rubbed Wanda's head.

Wanda mumbled a few unintelligible words about being foolish enough to think Max was falling in love with her and naïve enough to believe he had been chaste during his medical mission. "I hate him for this, for making a fool out of me!" Then she regretted her words and melted into tears once again.

Galina sat up, pulling Wanda into a seated position with her.

"I'm going to make some tea. You sit tight and have a good cry. I'll be right back, OK?"

Wanda nodded. Tears continued their path down her cheeks but with less fury than a few minutes earlier. Her thoughts settled too, less cluttered and more organized in her mind. *You're in love with him, that's the problem. Otherwise, you wouldn't care this much.* And that thought sickened her. How much easier it would be if it was only a matter of hurt pride and rejection.

Galina brought her tea and toast. Even through her stuffy nose, she had smelled the toast, its buttery aroma filling the air. Galina always remembered her favorite comfort food. But now, as Wanda stared at the plate, she doubted she could swallow anything. Galina pulled a pearl-colored chair up to the bedside.

"Just a little taste." Galina coaxed her, breaking off a tiny corner and setting it in her hand. "You don't want to leave your stomach empty of food with red wine sloshing around in there."

Wanda took a bite, an effort to appease her friend more than herself, and then swallowed a mouthful of Earl Grey.

"Have you heard from him?" Galina's voice was gentle.

Wanda nodded. "A couple of text messages."

"What did he say?"

Wanda, who had memorized the words, told her.

"You should give him the benefit of the doubt,

Wanda. Maybe it isn't as extreme as you imagine."

Wanda smirked. "That's wishful thinking."

"Why?"

"It seems more likely that it's bad. I'm sure that woman—Justine—wouldn't cause a scene over some guy she hardly knows."

"So you know her then? And you understand her motivations?"

"No." Wanda wanted to believe Galina. She wanted to believe Max. But she was too afraid of taking the risk. This taste of heartbreak was bad enough.

"You don't have to make a decision now but think about it. Before you cut Max out of your life without even letting him explain himself, think about it."

Wanda nodded, her energy spent. Galina left with the tea tray a few minutes later, and as soon as Wanda curled up against the pillows, she was asleep.

Chapter 21

Wanda spent the rest of her weekend dodging Max's calls and messages. She hid out at Galina's place, knowing that if she dared go home, Max would show up at her door.

"Doesn't that in and of itself prove he cares about you?" Galina had said.

She had a point, but Wanda refused to follow logic. She was too busy listening to her sentimental side.

Wanda could borrow a dress from Galina, meaning she wouldn't have to stop home before Monday. She left Nelly with Galina before heading to work, promising she would return home that night.

"You know you're welcome here," Galina had told her. "I just don't think you should be in flight mode too long. You have to return to reality."

Wanda walked to work, for the first time in months almost eager to get there. Anything to take her mind off Max and Justine.

Her enthusiasm about a day at Whilt was short-lived as she settled down behind her computer. Louis and Thomas approached her as she listened for voicemail.

She finished jotting down two calls to return and then turned to them.

"Wanda, Thomas was supposed to listen to an analyst call today but won't be able to do it," Louis said. "He's managed to line up a very important lunch with a CEO. So we need you to listen to the call and take notes for him."

"Isn't that what one of the assistants should be doing?" Wanda could feel her blood boil. Never in all of the years she'd been at Whilt had she ever asked a senior manager to listen to a routine analyst call for her. She knew the call Louis was referring to—and it wasn't anything important.

"Wanda, don't be a prima donna. Listening to an analyst call isn't beneath you."

"Fine," she said, then turned to Thomas. "Message me with the time and access codes, please."

He nodded and scurried off. He'd avoided speaking with Wanda lately. Perhaps he could read the ire on her face.

ॐ

Wanda dodged yet another happy hour with the laughing group who headed out the door as she was shutting down her computer. The "excuse" of having a baby to take care of was often ridiculed, so she simply said she had a headache. That did the trick.

Wanda let them leave first, several steps ahead on their way to the bar, and then hurried down the stairs and out the door. The cool evening air filled her lungs, and she shuddered as she clutched her black silk scarf against her throat.

"Wanda, finally." Max emerged from the shadows. "Give me a chance to explain." She took a step back, heart pounding. His eyes were imploring and wouldn't release hers. She stood speechless for an instant, then with every ounce of strength in her body and mind, she looked away and kept walking.

Max followed and quickly fell into step with her.

"Look, I don't need to hear it, OK?"

"Justine and I were on the mission together," he began.

Wanda blinked her eyes to hold back the tears. She should stop right now and hail a cab, but the taxis were all full at this hour. Or she should escape into that bar ahead. No, that was where her colleagues had gone for drinks. She should speed up her pace, but that was impossible in her high-heeled boots. So she sighed and stopped, turning to him.

"Fine," she said between clenched teeth. "Continue. Tell me everything. Tell me about how you played me for a fool from start to finish. Make me feel just great. I could use it right now."

He placed his hands gently on her shoulders, but she shrugged them off. He sighed.

"After you and I lost touch, Justine and I started seeing each other. Not immediately after, but little by little. We spent most of our days together so... I wanted to forget you. I tried hard to forget about you and figured a relationship with Justine was a good way to start. But it wasn't. It didn't feel right. At least not to me. I wanted to break up with her when I left Africa, but she insisted on leaving things open, in case she decided to return to Paris."

Wanda listened, unmoving. A small spark of hope, of joy, ignited within her heart, but she squelched it. Words were words. Max could say anything he wanted to appease her at this point.

"I told her I couldn't commit to her and left it at that," he continued. "The next time I saw her was with you at the party."

Wanda thought back to herself, pregnant with his baby as he was off fooling around with Justine. *But he didn't know! And you stopped calling him!* It was reasonable for him to continue living, wasn't it? But she couldn't let Max off the hook so easily. *Trying to forget about me by finding a new girlfriend? Yeah, right!*

"What do you expect me to do now?" Wanda snapped. She saw the pain in his eyes and wanted to believe it was sincere. But if she decided to trust him, she would be putting her heart in jeopardy.

"Wanda, I care about you—not Justine. Things are so good between us. I don't want to throw that away."

Wanda dropped her gaze to her toes. If she continued looking into his eyes, she would break down. She had to be firm.

"I've heard what you had to say. Now, I need some time. You clearly were able to jump from our relationship into another one quickly enough—"

"Wanda, it wasn't like that."

She turned and continued to walk in the direction of her apartment. He walked by her side.

"Max, I can't make a quick decision. My life is complicated right now."

"OK, I'm not asking for immediate forgiveness."

"I'm not sure you've done anything requiring forgiveness," she said. "You didn't cheat on me if you thought our relationship was over. You just disappointed me, looking for refuge in another relationship when ours was left in limbo. And I guess that's sometimes just as bad. But maybe all of this was my fault too. I didn't seek out a definite breakup either."

"It's not your fault." He took her hand, and she let him hold it for an instant, savoring the feel of his hand around hers, protecting it from the cold.

At the foot of her building, they turned to face each other.

"Can I come by to see you and Nelly this weekend?"
She nodded and then hurried through the door.

Chapter 22

The letter did not bring good news. Whilt Investment Services was cutting Wanda Julienne's salary by twenty percent because she had failed to meet goals in due time. Wanda's hands shook as she read the letter over and over, as if the words would magically change into something less catastrophic if she read them one more time.

That bastard! She thought of Louis but then remembered her earlier realization: He was a powerless fool, a messenger delivering information to and from management. He'd told Raymond Grant and the other New York bosses about her fund performance and her decision to reject the Asian funds, but he wasn't the one deciding how to punish her.

Still, Louis was her only point of contact, so, as usual, he was the one who met with her ire the next morning as she stood before him, letter in hand.

"I don't understand, Louis," she said between clenched teeth. "You saw the improvement in my funds—and in an extremely short period of time. One week beyond the impossible deadline you gave me."

"I'm not in control of those decisions, Wanda." He shrugged and slouched back into his chair. "Technically, you didn't meet the goal. You were a week late." He grinned.

"You've got to be kidding me," she said.

"The decision could always be reversed if I realize you are indeed amazing. And I bet you could be…" His voice trailed off, and his eyes seemed to unravel her sweater.

But Wanda was over being shocked by his comments. Ignoring them was the best weapon.

"Would management be satisfied if I obtained information illegally like some of my colleagues?" she asked.

"I don't know what you're talking about." He wrinkled his brow in feigned confusion.

"Of course you won't admit it. How silly of me to think you would."

"This letter is about you, Wanda—not about your colleagues."

"Right. The confidentiality thing."

"If you want more information about your situation, you can send a message to HR."

"So you're washing your hands of everything? You couldn't be the one to tell me about this even though I see you every day? I had to wait to receive this letter."

"That's the way things work around here, Wanda. You've been with Whilt long enough to know."

And that's where he was right.

๑๛

The pay cut would begin in exactly one month. Wanda didn't have to take out a calculator to know she was being priced out of her apartment. It might not have been a very big place, but it was in an excellent location.

Breaking the lease wasn't a concern. An apartment like this one would find a new occupant in a day.

What broke her heart was the idea of leaving, not only the apartment she had lived in for so many years, but also the neighborhood. She wouldn't find anything around here for less, which would mean a longer commute and more time away from Nelly. Then she thought of the nanny. She couldn't give up Colette, who was so good with Nelly. On her way to work, she would have to bring Nelly back to the building for the nanny share. Add another fifteen minutes to the morning clock. Tears rolled down her cheeks as she huddled into the corner of the couch and scrolled through apartment listings.

She hadn't told Galina, who would offer her money. She didn't want to depend on her friend. She didn't want to feel helpless. She would tell her after she had moved out of this apartment and into a new one, after she had managed on her own.

Through her tears, she calculated her other expenses. It was tight, but she and Nelly would scrape by.

Chapter 23

Attorney Daniel Lambert recommended writing Whilt a letter. It would be an attempt to address the problems, discuss them and find a solution. Wanda sat at the edge of her seat, eager and naïve, as Lambert questioned her across his cluttered desk. It was the only cluttered thing in the room, that heavy mahogany structure sitting between them. Otherwise, the place was light and airy, with white sculpted walls, a cathedral ceiling and an absence of furnishings. Wanda almost felt her voice echoing as she asked a question or replied to one.

"The discrimination is flagrant," Lambert finally said, gazing at her over the rim of his glasses. "And from what you said, it's clear there was sexual harassment. But that doesn't mean it will be an easy battle in the courtroom."

"What do you mean?"

"We need solid proof."

"And what I have isn't proof?"

"I've been in this business for thirty years, Ms. Julienne, and I've had cases that seemed infallible. And those were often the cases I lost."

Wanda felt a shiver run up and down her spine. Was he trying to discourage her? Why had Galina sent her here? Wanda should have listened to her own instinct. She should have cut her losses and quit. It would have been over by now and maybe she would have even found another job.

"You're probably wondering why I'm telling you that," Lambert said, interrupting her thoughts.

"Yes, as a matter of fact."

"Just because something seems obvious to you or to me doesn't mean it is legally sound."

"You mean I don't have a case?" Wanda almost wished he would confirm her fears. At least that way, she would know where she stood.

"I didn't say that. Never assume anything."

"What are you saying then?"

"That discrimination, that harassment, require a number of supporting elements, including affidavits and preferably witnesses."

Wanda bit her lip as images of her colleagues suddenly blinded her. She saw them laughing, gossiping, burrowed behind computers or chatting in the kitchen. She saw Flora criticizing her for no longer playing the singles game even though she still was single. She heard Sam laughing at her for refusing a glass of wine because she was too damned tired. Would any of these people actually make a statement on her behalf? Not a judgment of whether there had been misconduct, but simply a statement of fact. If one did, he or she would be next on Whilt's list.

"You see where I'm going with this," Lambert said as if reading her mind. "Gathering evidence is up to you— and you will find it to be a challenging endeavor."

Wanda walked out of the office with a notebook full of recommendations and a plan of action. Lambert would address a letter to Whilt, an attempt at reconciliation. Whilt's response would determine whether the next step would be a friendly agreement or litigation.

The evening chill had set in as she walked down the street, passing cafés serving cocktails to the early crowd. Strangely, in spite of the dreadful evidence-gathering task awaiting her, she felt rather serene. At least she had made a decision, taken a step. And at least Lambert had confirmed that she did indeed have a case. Now, she just had to prove it to the judge.

Her phone rang, and she fumbled in her bag until she saw Colette's name flashing on the screen. Not a call to ignore. She answered breathlessly.

"Don't worry, everything's OK," Colette said. "I'm just calling to say the doctor is late so Nelly and I are still stuck in the office. I'm thinking we'll be here for another hour."

"I can try to meet you there."

"No, don't worry about it. By the time you get here, we'll probably be inside with the doctor."

"So I guess this means I don't have to rush to get her," Wanda said with a sigh of relief. She had expected to be a half hour late, but now it was looking as if she would make it back to the apartment well before they did. "Thanks for letting me know, Colette."

"No prob! Enjoy your free time." Wanda could almost see Colette's smile on the other end of the line. Colette was a jewel of a nanny. Wanda would eat potatoes every day if she had to, just to afford keeping Nelly in Colette's care.

So Wanda's rapid footsteps slowed to a calmer pace, a strolling pace that she rarely had time to savor. Another café, this one with heat lamps warming the bravest of patrons who chose to sit outside. As Wanda gazed at the picturesque scene, her heart skipped a beat. She froze to the spot even though all she wanted to do was run. There, right before her, sat Max and Justine. Each bundled in a warm coat, each with a hand wrapped around a cup of coffee, each wearing a serious expression. So involved were they in conversation that it seemed odd that Max, right then, looked up, straight into Wanda's eyes. It was as if he had sensed her presence.

Wanda took a step back and then another.

"Wanda!" He rose from his seat, but she was already a few steps ahead.

"Wait," he called out.

"Max, what's going on?" Justine's voice echoed in the distance.

Wanda wished she hadn't worn her high-heeled boots. They were a liability, slowing her just enough so that Max could catch up, grab her by the arms and turn her around to face him. He was in a panic, his eyes flashing with concern.

"Wanda, please, I can explain!"

Wanda wrenched herself out of his grip and turned away, but he easily kept up with her rapid steps.

"It looks as if Justine isn't as out of the picture as you made it seem." Wanda was annoyed with herself for letting the hurt and anger seep through. Why couldn't she be cool and indifferent instead of excitable and emotional?

"Wanda, we have to talk."

Those simple words sliced through her heart like a knife. She could either keep walking and push him away or face him and whatever he had to say. She continued a few steps, slowing a bit, as she considered her options. And then she stopped. No use in running. Better off knowing right away that he didn't love her.

"OK, what is it?" She faced him, arms crossed against her chest, heavy bag falling to her elbow. They stood in the middle of the busy sidewalk, illuminated by street lamps and a light drizzle that had begun to fall. His eyes were somber and intense, more black than brown.

"Let's sit down somewhere—"

"The middle of the street is fine for this conversation, Max." Her voice was decisive.

He looked down and sighed. Wanda held her breath, bracing herself for the hurtful words.

"I asked Justine to meet me for a drink because I wanted to end things officially," he said. "I want to be with you and Nelly."

"She wants to get back together, right?"

"It doesn't matter what she wants."

Wanda wanted to believe him. Any person whose mind wasn't in turmoil would have accepted his words, would have trusted his intentions. But Wanda had lost faith. She was scared and doubtful. Was Max's decision out of true love or obligation? He wasn't one to shirk his duties, and she didn't want to be a charity case.

"Look, we should just stop this right here," Wanda said. "You don't have to stay with me because of Nelly. Just live your life the way you want to, with the person you want to be with. And forget about me, forget about us."

She saw the pain in his eyes when she pronounced those words, but she couldn't help herself. And this time, she turned and ran. No matter how high those heels were, no matter how slippery the sidewalks, she ran.

Chapter 24

Wanda's new apartment was in the tenth arrondissement, a working class area with direct subway access to the office and her nanny share. She'd darted to apartment visits on her lunch break every day for two weeks and finally settled after realizing her new salary wasn't going to afford her great luxury. A small humid studio, a walkup off a noisy boulevard. The one positive was it was on the top floor, which meant it would be calm without the heavy footsteps of renters above. The apartment was under the rafters—like Max's. But she tried not to think of that. She had successfully ignored his calls for a week. She had ignored his visits too, remaining silent with only the door separating them.

But today wasn't about Max. It was about Galina, who had become so impatient with Wanda's evasiveness that she'd paid her a surprise visit. And found her packing. She'd arrived just as Wanda had opened the door to cart a trash bag downstairs.

Wanda drew in a sharp breath as Galina dropped her purse to the floor and scanned the room.

"What on earth is going on here?" As usual, she was

calm, but Wanda could sense the tension in her voice. There would be no inventing stories. That wouldn't work face-to-face with Galina. There would only be truth.

Wanda left the bag in the vestibule and led Galina into the living room. Boxes covered the floor, picture frames lay against the couch, and dust bunnies gathered in the corners, exposed by all of the activity.

"Where's Nelly?" Galina asked, her dark eyes wide.

"Napping in her room."

Galina slipped out of her soft gray cloak and folded it neatly on the back of the couch before sitting down.

"Go ahead," she said. "I'm listening."

Wanda collapsed at her feet, and the whole story of the past few weeks spewed out in an incoherent mess that only her best friend would understand. From Whilt to Max to the apartment search—her body expelled each detail as if ridding itself of poison.

"I would have helped you stay here," Galina said. "I'm suspecting that's why you didn't tell me."

Wanda nodded, and Galina handed her a tissue to mop up the tears.

"What's done is done. I'm not going to chastise you, even though I think it was foolish of you to turn away from me and refuse my help before I was able to offer it."

"I know. It's just that you shouldn't have to keep sweeping up the debris of my life."

"I don't see it that way."

"I wanted—want—to handle this on my own."

"And you have, and it's fine, Wanda. But I'll miss waving to you from across the way."

"Me too," Wanda whispered. She didn't want to be in the new place, that tiny space far from the neighborhood she knew, far from her best friend. But she had chosen independence, and it was the right choice. That, at least, erased some of the pain.

"You saw Lambert, right? He's handling the situation."

Wanda nodded. She wanted to say, *I wish you had taken the case*, but she realized that opting for independence meant she had to stop begging her friend for help—legal or otherwise.

"Max called me," Galina said.

"What?" Wanda's heart pounded at the sound of his name.

"Well, when he tried to reach you in every way imaginable and each attempt failed, he had to find a Plan B."

"Plan B?"

"Another way to achieve the goal." Galina looked at her pointedly.

"Yeah, I *know* what a Plan B is, I just couldn't imagine it being applied to me."

"Well it was—is."

Wanda remained silent, twirling a few loose strands from the rug between her fingers.

"Aren't you going to ask me what he said? Aren't you curious?"

"I shouldn't. I shouldn't be. I mean after—"

"He cares about you, Wanda. Can't you see that?"

"Oh really? Look at how fast he found a replacement for me when he was on his mission!"

"Wanda... Come on. You stopped calling him. You argued with him most of the time when you did talk."

"Yeah, I know. But he recovered fast enough!"

"You don't know the nature of the relationship."

"So what do you expect me to do?"

"Give him a chance."

"I'll think about it." Wanda's words were empty, and she knew Galina was smart enough to realize this. Galina also was smart enough to know it wasn't the time to push Wanda.

"So when is the move?" she asked instead.

"In a week."

"How are you managing?"

"I took a few days off work. I couldn't do it otherwise."

"I mean for all of your stuff."

"Xavier and a few of his friends." Heat rose into Wanda's cheeks, a reflection of her shame. She'd turned to casual friends while keeping her best friend in the dark. But Galina wasn't jealous or petty.

"I'm glad you found some help, but if you need Charles or me, just let us know, OK? In any case, we'll watch Nelly." She placed a delicate hand on Wanda's shoulder, and Wanda squeezed it.

Chapter 25

Whilt management had received the attorney's letter according to the return receipt ticket. Wanda waited for a phone call, a message, some sign of life. Nothing. And then, a few days before her move, Lambert called. Whilt had replied. The company denies any wrongdoing, any unfairness whatsoever, the letter to Lambert said. Wanda's heart sank, yet she wasn't surprised. Lambert had warned her that big corporations like Whilt never backed down—no matter how wrong they might be— and the case would end up in the courtroom.

"What have you decided to do, Ms. Julienne?" he asked.

"What choice do I have? We have to move forward."

That was how Wanda's homework turned from fund research to Whilt research. With her fund performance now positive, she no longer had to extend her workday into the night. So in the evening hours, she researched cases against Whilt—and there were plenty of them. For discrimination, salary problems, overtime issues. In some instances, the employee won, in others, the employee settled. In very few instances, Whilt came out victorious.

And according to Wanda's research, at least two other women were currently suing the company for sexual harassment and discrimination.

All of this was interesting, but none of it gave her the evidence she needed for her trial. She rubbed her bleary eyes as she shifted her laptop from her knees to the couch.

Why are you doing this? To get your mind off Max and losing your apartment and how your life is generally out of control? Is this a way of taking control? She pushed that voice of reason out of her mind.

Through all of her research, she couldn't find a thing about Kate, the former coworker who had supposedly been harassed by Louis. Wanda hadn't told her attorney or Galina about Kate. She wanted to be certain first. She'd tried to reach Kate already, leaving messages in a voice she wished wasn't so shaky. She still had Kate's cell phone number, as she had every Whilt Paris employee's number.

Wanda had left three messages in three days, and Kate had not returned her calls. The answer seemed clear: Kate was involved in her own case and wasn't interested in talking with Wanda. Still, she dared to hope. *Wait a bit longer. Maybe, just maybe, she'll come around.*

A small cry from Nelly startled Wanda, and she looked down at the baby wiggling in the lounger. She knelt and rubbed a chubby arm. Nelly squirmed, then settled back to sleep. The crying and clinginess that had followed Wanda's trips continued, making it almost impossible to put Nelly to sleep in her crib. Instead, Wanda rocked her to sleep in the lounger and then would transfer her to the crib much later, when she was in a deep sleep.

"I'm trying to be strong, and I'm fighting this battle for you, for us," she whispered in her sleeping daughter's ear. "Everything will be OK. You'll see."

Wanda wiped a tear from her eye as she studied Nelly's smooth cheeks and the small face that was somehow a complete reflection of Max. How could she push him out of her mind when she had this tiny reminder sitting in front of her every day?

She kissed Nelly's head, rubbing her lips against wispy curls, and stood up. It was only nine o'clock, and the baby hadn't been sleeping very long. It was too early for the transfer.

Wanda was about to return to her computer when a knock at the door startled her. She hurried across the floor. She didn't have to look out the peephole to know Max was on the other side. If he kept knocking, Nelly would wake up, and hysteria was almost guaranteed.

Wanda couldn't avoid this confrontation forever. Again, he'd waited outside her office a few days ago, but this time, she'd spotted him ahead of time. She'd snuck out the back door, then scolded herself for immature behavior. And that was another factor encouraging her to face him. It was time to grow up, to be bold enough to turn him away rather than running away herself.

"Wanda." She loved the sound of her name when he pronounced it. Then she cringed. No. She couldn't be this weak right from the start. She took a step back, leaving a fair distance between them.

"C'mon in."

"You're moving?"

"Looks like it."

"Could I ask why?"

"A pay cut at Whilt means I can't afford this place."

"Wanda, you can't be serious."

"Oh but I am."

She was able to be glib about the situation from time to time. It was either that or panic—she vacillated between the two.

"I... I don't know what to say."

"There's nothing to say about it, Max. But you obviously have something to say about something else or you wouldn't be here. Want to sit down?"

He sank to the floor near Nelly and touched her cheek. She squirmed, then settled.

"Should we keep our voices down?"

"No, talking is fine. She needs another half hour, and she'll be out like a light." A small smile crept onto Wanda's face, then quickly disappeared.

"I've been trying to see you."

"I know."

"Why can't we give ourselves another chance, Wanda? Why are you punishing us this way?"

"It's not punishment." She rolled her eyes.

"We have a good thing, and you don't want to continue it. So yes, it is punishing."

He was right, of course, but Wanda was stubborn and not ready to trust him or anyone else—not even herself.

"I explained the situation to Justine that night you saw us at the café. She accepted the fact that it's over."

Wanda looked down at her hands, long lily white fingers that wore no rings. "You really don't want to be with me right now, Max. No one should be with me right now. Things are difficult."

"I know. The work situation—"

"Yes. I can't be... bothered with... a relationship. I have to wait until I can straighten things out in my professional life, move to a new place. It's just not the right time. I can't trust myself to judge how I feel and to understand how you feel." She said those words even though she ached to be with him, to have him as part of her life.

Wanda ran her fingers through her hair, forgetting that it was already tied back in a ponytail. A few strands fell loose, and Max leaned forward to push them back.

Wanda let his lips graze her ear, let herself shiver at his touch, then stood up.

"I allowed everything to get out of hand when I took off with you to Normandy. I shouldn't have done that."

"Wanda, it was wonderful! You can't regret it…"

"Yes, it was wonderful—if I don't think of the Justine element."

Max looked at her with sad eyes, wrenching her heart. "Wanda…"

"I have a serious situation on my hands with work. Look around, Max. These boxes, soon on their way to my cubbyhole apartment, were not meant to be here. They wouldn't be here if Whilt hadn't started this ridiculous process of elimination—eliminating employees for convenience rather than poor performance or economics. I need time to think, to be alone…" She said the words quickly, before her emotions could stop her.

Max stood next to Wanda, taking her hands in his.

"It would be so much better together."

She gazed at their hands, entwined so perfectly, and then let go.

Chapter 26

"Wait until they dive into Louis' family finances. They practically have pots of gold for dinner!"

"And what about Maddie? Her husband is absolutely loaded."

Flora and Sam were up to the usual gossip, leaning against the wall abutting Wanda's desk. The distraction annoyed her. Why did they always have to stop there, right at the corner, and talk over her head when she was trying to concentrate? She scowled at her computer screen and tried to block out their words—but soon, she heard her name.

"Wanda? Wanda?"

She looked up at the two, who now turned in her direction.

"Hmm?"

"Have you read the memo?" Flora hissed.

"What memo?"

"It was sent out to everyone an hour ago," Sam said. "Check your inbox."

They hovered over Wanda as she scrolled through her messages and clicked on it. She hated having them crowd her like this. She figured it best to get through this as quickly as possible if she hoped to get rid of them. She scanned the message, and then a strange feeling overcame her.

"Insane, isn't it?" Flora hissed, as if excited by the possibility of Wanda joining their gossip session. "What are they thinking?"

It was insane. The company had sent out a memo requiring employees to reveal all of their personal financial information. Whilt wasn't simply talking stocks and bonds. The company wanted to know the value of property held, bank accounts, inheritances and even financial gifts made to employees' children.

Wanda looked at her colleagues' eager faces. She didn't want to join in the behind-the-scenes chitchat only to meekly comply with management an hour later. Better to be looked at as an outsider from the start.

"I think the bigger question is 'Is this legal?'" Wanda said, knowing this would cut the conversation short. "Now is anyone going to get a lawyer to find out?"

Flora and Sam both blushed, and Wanda shrugged.

"I didn't mean to mention the big bad word: 'lawyer.' Sorry about that. Now, I have to get back to this report, so if you'll excuse me."

"Sure," Flora said, biting her lip. She and Sam looked at each other, then turned and walked in opposite directions back to their desks.

"Whilt should pay me to cut down on office gossip," Wanda muttered. But she didn't immediately return to her report. Instead, she examined the memo more closely. What did this mean? Asking about stock and bond holdings was understandable. But requiring an employee to reveal how much money his or her house was worth didn't have anything to do with Whilt business.

Wanda didn't have riches to hide. As a matter of fact,

what she was most ashamed of was her lack of money. Her salary would now be enough to cover food and lodging—considering she was about to move into a small, cheap apartment. What was there even to declare to Whilt?

She made a mental note that she would refuse to make any declaration to the company. She would hold her head high and remain proud no matter what the consequences. Wanda refused to bow down, to bend to a senseless idea because she knew that wouldn't save her job. The day Whilt wanted her out, she would be out.

৯৵৶

Maddie was holding her head in her hands when Wanda rapped gently on her office door and stepped inside.

"Everything OK?"

Maddie looked up with a wan smile.

"I have a difficult decision," she said.

"I'm sorry to hear that." Wanda grimaced. She'd intended to ask Maddie for some help digging up evidence. She hadn't expected to find her in a crisis of her own. "Is there anything I can do?"

"Everything will be fine, everything will work out," Maddie said, her usual look of self-assurance returning. "It always has in the past. Now what can I help you with, Wanda?"

"I can come back another time—"

"No, no, this is fine." Maddie stood up, brushing off her camel-colored suit, and walked around her desk to sit next to Wanda on the other side. "I need a distraction today."

Wanda took a deep breath and stared at her hands, trembling in her lap. She hadn't realized she would be so nervous. She had to get this over with if she hoped to ever have a shot in the courtroom.

"Maddie, I'm planning on suing the company."

"An understandable decision. And you're not the first."

"You're not shocked?"

"Maybe a little surprised that you, the calm, hardworking Wanda Julienne are making an aggressive move."

Wanda smirked. "I didn't want to. I'm at the point of not having much of a choice. When unfairness reaches a certain level…"

"I know I encouraged you to fight, and it's the right decision. But I feel I have to warn you too. You have to understand what you're getting into, Wanda, poking around the hornets' nest. They won't make things easy for you around here."

"That's all right. Things haven't been easy since I returned from maternity leave. It's as if the whole company changed while I was gone."

"You know my views on that, Wanda. The company didn't change. You did. You now have a baby, a different lifestyle."

"You're right. This sort of thing was happening to others long before me, and I didn't even notice or care. I'm ashamed of that, the fact that I didn't care."

Maddie shrugged. "You can't take on the problems of the world, Wanda."

"I know, but I wish I'd been more understanding of some of the other women. Like when Kate would refuse our drinks invitations."

"Is that what you came here to chat about, Wanda?" Maddie narrowed her eyes. "Somehow, I don't think so."

Wanda hesitated and then opened her mouth to continue even as her heart pounded double time.

"It has to do with my case. I need some evidence, Maddie. I need someone else to testify about… well, a bunch of things. The way they gave me unrealistic goals for my funds, yet didn't even punish Thomas for ruining their performance in the first place. The harassment. I've tried contacting Kate, but she hasn't returned my calls."

"Those are private matters between you and management, Wanda. You'll never get someone to speak on your behalf. Even though Kate had a similar problem, who knows what strategy she and her lawyer are using? Her lawyer might have advised her not to talk with anyone."

Wanda's heart sank as Maddie's words echoed all of the fears that had run through her mind.

"In the Whilt environment, you can be sure it's almost impossible to gather witnesses. Everyone around here looks after themselves."

"Including you?" The words flew out of Wanda's mouth before she could stop them. She hadn't wanted to ask Maddie that question, hadn't wanted to face the fact that even she would turn her back and leave Wanda to face the sharks on her own.

"I'm sorry, Wanda." She dropped her gaze and shook her head. "I would, but I have to think of my position."

"Why do you want to hang onto this job so much, Maddie?" Wanda snapped, anger managing to mask the hurt. "You aren't desperate for money like I am! You aren't being forced to move to a broom closet with your baby because they unjustly cut your salary."

Her words hung in the air, like a banner separating the two women.

"Wanda," Maddie whispered. But Wanda wasn't in the mood to listen. She hurried from the room before the tears could fall.

Chapter 27

Wanda walked through her empty apartment. Xavier and his friends had loaded up a truck with boxes and were on their way to the new place. Wanda would drop the keys off at the rental agency and then take the subway over. She lingered in Nelly's room, remembering the day she first set the baby in her crib. Wanda could still hear Brahms' Lullaby as the pink mobile with yellow stars danced over the baby's head.

She gazed out the window at the naked plane trees that had been so lush on that summer day. She couldn't have imagined then that less than a year later her life would be in such turmoil. She couldn't have imagined that Galina would be babysitting not because Wanda was at work or running errands—but because Wanda was moving.

She went through the rooms one by one, as flashes of memory assaulted her, their warmth chilling her bones. The bedroom she had first split with Galina during those early days in Paris, then shared with Max on so many warm summer nights. That spot in the living room, in a beanbag chair near the fireplace, where she would curl up with a good book, back in the days when she had time for leisure reading.

But what brought her to tears was the bay window overlooking the city. Not for the Eiffel Tower view, but for the connection with Galina, the feeling that she could wave, and her best friend would be there, on the other side of the tower, waving back. It was as if, by walking out the door for the last time, she was cutting the tie. She cried for a while, then glanced at her watch and dried her eyes. She couldn't stay here all day, pathetic and miserable, while Xavier unloaded her boxes across town. She went through a package of tissues, then took enough deep breaths to restore some sense of calm, even if only temporarily.

Wanda's effort worked just long enough to complete the task. She held onto her tears as she ran down the stairs, hurried along the street and dropped her keys at the rental agency. Then she stepped back onto the sidewalk, put on her sunglasses on a sunless day, and let them flow.

ৡঞ

"It's kind of cute," Rita said as Wanda crossed the threshold. Rita had her curly hair piled up on top of her head and was wearing a pair of ripped jeans and one of Xavier's old shirts. She had been sliding boxes into one corner of the apartment, freeing up space for the men to assemble the beds and dresser drawers. Thankfully, Wanda didn't have much furniture. Her old apartment had always looked a bit sparse; this one would look full.

"You don't have to do all this," Wanda said as she kissed Rita on both cheeks. "I didn't realize you would be here too, especially since you're just in Paris for a few days."

"Are you kidding? Wanda, we know what you're

going through at Whilt. We can't do much for you other than this, after the settlement. So we'll do what we can."

Xavier came over and patted her on the back, congratulating her for not owning as many heavy decorative objects as Rita. Rita took a swipe at him as he darted off, and Wanda grinned. She knew they were trying their hardest to lighten up the situation, and she appreciated it. They had seen her red, swollen eyelids when she'd taken off her sunglasses.

She gazed at the room from end to end. An alcove in one corner for their beds, a bathroom tucked into another corner and the rest one room with an open kitchen. Windows overhead let in streams of light even on a dark day.

"It's so bright," Rita said, as if reading her mind. "You know, it's difficult to find an apartment that looks this cheerful even in early February."

But it was cramped. Enough room for Nelly to crawl and learn to walk, but beyond that... No, Wanda couldn't think beyond that, couldn't imagine they would spend that long in such a tiny place on such a noisy street.

"Bright, but meant for one person, not two," she said.

"If things get uncomfortable, come stay with us for the weekend, OK?"

Rita and Xavier were moving to a farmhouse in the Loire Valley. With plenty of bedrooms and a vast expanse of greenery beyond, the offer was tempting. But it wasn't a solution by any means.

"Maybe a visit will do us good at some point, thanks," Wanda said, sinking onto the couch that her friends had just placed behind her. "But we have to find our way out of this situation permanently."

"You realize that means you'll have to leave Whilt?"

"It'll happen—one way or another." She had told

Rita and Xavier of her plan to sue the company. "The problem is the job market. It's so bad. That's why I've stayed with Whilt all this time. What other options are there?"

"Moving entirely? Have you thought of going back to the U.S.?"

Max. That was her first thought, and she felt an embarrassing blush rise into her cheeks. She was driving him away, yet she refused to leave Paris because of him. And it wasn't because she was thinking of his visits with Nelly. Plenty of divorced parents lived on separate continents and sent the children back and forth for vacations. No, she was thinking she couldn't imagine her life without Max. Yet every time he got too close, she pushed him away. *What's wrong with you?*

"Wanda?"

"Yeah, sorry. No, I don't want to leave. Not now. Plus, the economy there is suffering too."

Rita slumped onto the couch next to her. "It's not a pretty picture, is it? Being at the mercy of a merciless company. One minute you're doing well, treated properly and paid properly, and then the next, you're in a downward spiral."

"You sound as if you know what you're talking about."

Rita smirked. "I've seen it happen a lot—"

"OK, you two, we've finished our part of the job," Xavier interrupted.

"Don't worry about anything else," Wanda said quickly as she jumped to her feet. "Everyone, go home and enjoy the rest of the day. I can handle things from here."

Chapter 28

Louis called her into his office bright and early, which for him was about eleven a.m. Her heart had taken to racing every time a message from Louis or the human resources department appeared in her inbox. A Pavlovian response. Every bit of communication since her return from maternity leave had been negative in one way or another.

Wanda adjusted her silk blouse over her gray trousers so she didn't look quite so rumpled after several hours behind her desk. She smoothed back her hair and glanced at her reflection in the mirrored elevator. She had lost weight and turned pale, and now sported dark circles under her eyes that no amount of concealer could cover. She sighed and looked away, preferring the view of her feet in black patent leather.

Wanda marched into Louis' office, startling him even though he should have been expecting her.

"This shouldn't be a surprise," she said, taking a seat.

He walked around the desk and sat in the chair next to hers.

"I didn't expect you to be prompt, Wanda. Deadlines

haven't been your thing lately."

She ignored his comment. "You wanted to see me about something?"

"You haven't filled out your financial disclosure paperwork. See what I meant about deadlines?"

"I've decided not to fill it out."

"Well how do you expect management to get the information, babe? By osmosis?"

"Hopefully not. Because my personal financial information isn't Whilt's business."

"Hmm, another one of your decisions?" He shot her a patronizing look, his cool blue eyes icier than ever. "It doesn't work that way around here. You should understand that, Wanda. How can you expect to remain part of Whilt if you're constantly fighting the system?"

"Is that a threat, Louis?" she asked, her heart pounding a mile a minute. She hoped the heat in her face hadn't turned into a blush of embarrassment.

"A simple observation and maybe a bit of advice too." He shrugged. "You can't say no to Whilt. Things are the way they are around here and won't change. The company has a good reason for asking what it does of its employees."

"OK, then, what is it? Why should I declare, for instance, how much money my parents have put in a college fund for my child?"

"Only Whilt can say. You can send a message to HR with your question."

"This is a violation of privacy. Whilt can't gain complete, unfettered access to every aspect of my life."

"Then be prepared for the consequences. And don't say I didn't warn you."

Another shrug and he stood up, returning to his side of the desk.

ଚ୬

Wanda arrived home at the new apartment no earlier than seven-thirty every night, and that was only if she managed to leave the office at six-thirty on the dot. So some nights, eight o'clock was more likely. If this was all about her, she wouldn't have cared. But for Nelly, the new schedule was rough. On most evenings, she wailed the whole subway ride, eagerly slurped down her bottle at home, fussed in the bathtub and finally fell into a deep but often agitated sleep. By about nine o'clock, Wanda was able to curl up on the couch with her laptop and a bowl of takeout noodles.

On this particular evening, her second week in the apartment, a soft knocking on the door interrupted her as she sat down. She tiptoed across the room and released the latch. She drew in a deep breath when she saw Max.

"How did you know—?"

"Galina gave me your address," he said. "Hope you don't mind." Her eyes locked with his, unable and unwilling to escape.

He held out a bouquet of pink roses. "Happy Valentine's Day. I just got off work, or I would have come by earlier."

"Max, I... Thank you." The apartment was drafty, but all of a sudden she felt as if her body temperature had surged well over a hundred degrees.

"Should I stay out here in the hallway?" he asked with the half grin that made her heart flip flop.

"No. Sorry. Come in. I didn't even realize today was a holiday. Life has been kind of crazy."

"You mean you haven't noticed the red hearts in every window display?" he asked.

"My eyes are usually directed at the sidewalk."

Wanda took his coat, inhaling the scent of him as she tossed it over a hook on the back of the door. Max glanced around at the array of half unpacked boxes, then quickly found Nelly's crib. He knelt at its side, smiling, while Wanda grabbed her only vase off a shelf, filled it with water and arranged the flowers.

She shouldn't have let him in. He would break her down, and this was the first step. But was she that weak? She could handle a few platonic encounters, couldn't she? Wanda couldn't keep Max out of Nelly's life forever. And she didn't want to.

Max joined her on the couch, and she lifted up her plate and handed him a fork.

"If you haven't eaten yet?"

He smiled. "I should have thought of that. How about if I call for something? There's that pizza place downstairs. I know it's not the most elegant Valentine's dinner—"

"It doesn't have to be. Remember, we don't have a reason to celebrate Valentine's Day." She tried to convince herself as much as she tried to convince him.

An hour later, they were sharing a pizza, and an hour after that, they were in Wanda's bed.

Chapter 29

A dull routine set in, carrying Wanda from February to mid-March. The wakeup routine, long subway rides, dropping off Nelly, work, retrieving Nelly, another subway ride, home, sleep. The monotony was punctuated by a few evenings with Galina, but she kept them as infrequent as possible. She was exhausted physically and mentally. She avoided Max altogether. She left him a message saying their night together had been a mistake, and she apologized for her own weakness, for letting raw emotions drive her at a time when so much turmoil cluttered her mind.

"I didn't mean to manipulate you," she'd said into the phone. "You're better off without me and all of my baggage."

Lambert filed suit against Whilt on Wanda's behalf, and the case was officially out of her hands. Work continued, and Wanda looked for any excuse to meet with clients outside of the office or attend conferences that would take her far from Louis' leering eye or messages from the human resources department, insisting she reveal her finances and accept the Asian funds.

As Wanda read the latest email, she muttered to herself, *Maybe I should just do it. Maybe I should do anything they want.*

The only thing holding her back from revealing her finances was shame. Shame that after all of these years at Whilt, she was two paychecks away from homelessness. Wanda had very little to her name, and she didn't exactly want Whilt upper management to know just how badly she needed her job.

That was probably Whilt's motive with this new rule: to see how many high salary earners were close to poverty if Whilt booted them out the door. That would give the company plenty of leverage.

Wanda realized she probably wasn't the only one. A lot of her colleagues lived up to and well beyond their means. Or perhaps the company realized the high earners would rather leave than drop to their knees before Big Brother. An easy way to streamline the budget. But this was all supposition, and Wanda didn't care about Whilt's motives. She just knew that she wouldn't bend—no matter what. If the company did fire her, she would receive meager unemployment benefits, but she and Nelly would manage.

Wanda ran into Max in front of her building the first evening she shed her heavy winter coat for a lightweight beige trench. Spring was in the air. Max had come to her door several times before, but she hadn't answered. Now, he faced her with sadness in his eyes, a sadness that had been clearly growing for weeks. Guilt and shame consumed her, but she refused to lower the wall of defense she had erected to protect herself from more pain.

"Can I come in?" he asked.

She nodded. He helped her up the stairs with Nelly and held the baby while Wanda took off her shoes and prepared a bottle. She heard him whispering and singing to Nelly, then heard the baby's laugh, and tears sprang into her eyes. All of this was Whilt's fault. If she wasn't going through this, she would be able to live a normal life and focus on relationships rather than court cases and harassment.

She wiped her eyes, blew her nose, took a deep, calming breath, and turned back to father and daughter.

"You OK?" Max asked.

"Allergies," she replied. "Everything is in bloom, or almost."

Wanda set the bottle back on the counter. Nelly was dozing in Max's arms.

"Here, let's get her settled in the lounger," Wanda said. "I can wake her in a half hour for her milk if she doesn't wake up earlier."

"Must have had a tiring day with the nanny and friends," Max said as he gently lowered her into the sling. Wanda strapped her in, and then she and Max stood up.

"So what did you want to see me about?" She sounded frightened, yet another attempt at nonchalance failed.

"To give you this." Max held out a check for enough money to cover a month's rent.

She knitted her eyebrows. "What's this for?"

"Nelly is my daughter, Wanda. I should be contributing." His eyes brightened; he was obviously pleased with this initiative.

"No, there's no reason for that. There's no reason to feel sorry for us or—" Her heartbeat quickened as a rush of emotions collided within. Happiness that Max cared and recognized his responsibility but sorrow about what this might confirm: Perhaps this was all about fulfilling a duty and nothing more. *Is this pity? Is it because we look desperate?*

"This isn't about feeling sorry for you." His voice

was firm. "I went to the city hall this morning and declared paternity. I'm now required to offer you financial support, and I want to. If I didn't want to, I wouldn't have made this official."

Joy should have overwhelmed Wanda, convincing her that Max was in love with her, was in love with them. And that feeling tried to rush through her, but an even more powerful emotion violently blocked it: fear. Fear that Max was jumping in too quickly and would regret his decision.

"Is everything OK?" Max continued. "I thought this would prove my feelings and commitment to both of you."

Wanda turned and walked toward the window, her hands to her head. Max followed close behind. She turned to face him, wanting to fall into his arms but instead taking a step back.

"What is it, Wanda?" he insisted.

She took a deep breath, and looked into his eyes and the confusion that had replaced the sparkle of only a few minutes ago.

"I appreciate the effort, Max, and thank you for it, but I think we should have talked about it before you went ahead and declared paternity. Why didn't you ask me?"

"Wanda, that's ridiculous! I'm the father so I have the right to declare myself as such."

"I didn't mean it that way." She shook her head in frustration. "I'm saying it's an important step and right now isn't the time."

"It *is* the time, Wanda," he snapped. "Look around. If you don't need me and can handle yourself so well, why are you living in this dump and eating takeout noodles every day? This isn't any way to raise Nelly, even for a little while! Especially when you have a choice."

Wanda flew into a fury, her pride wounded by those

words not because of their strength but because of their veracity. She would defend herself. She refused to believe he was right.

"What do you know about raising a child, Max? How dare you try to assert control over us, over this situation!" She snatched the check from his hands and ripped it in two. "And that's what I think of your money!"

Max looked at her blankly, then shook his head.

"Wanda," he started to say. But she stared at him with an expression icier than even those she'd used when facing Louis.

"No. Just leave."

"I can't believe you. This is selfish. It's become all about you and your pride rather than what really would be best for you and Nelly. How long are you going to push me away, Wanda?"

"I don't need you to look after us." She was shaking with anger now—but not all of the anger was directed at Max. Much of it was directed at herself, for being so proud, so fearful, that she just might be pushing away everything she should cherish.

Max stalked out the door and slammed it, shaking the whole apartment. Nelly woke with a moan that rose to a shrill cry, like a siren in the night.

Chapter 30

Registered mail had rarely brought good news in Wanda's life. She remembered the time she was evicted from her off-campus apartment during college and received the letter explaining the development project. Then there was her father's demotion as he reached the end of his career in education; a cold, simple envelope that he held for a long while, knowing what it contained.

For Wanda, this registered letter was no exception. Even before she opened the envelope, her hands shook.

It was a Whilt envelope, with the company logo embossed in the usual royal blue. Normally, she wouldn't have been around to receive it, but instead of spending the day at the office, she was spending the day sick in bed. "Exhaustion, physical and mental," the doctor had said, prescribing a cocktail of pills and ordering her to stay home for at least two days.

Slowly, Wanda unsealed the envelope, unfolded the letter inside and scanned the page. Whilt was firing her. Her refusal to manage the new funds and her refusal to declare her finances meant she was not complying with company policy, and her fund performance was

unsatisfactory. She was instructed not to return to the
office. She would receive a box with her belongings in
the coming days.

Her stomach tied itself in knots as she read the letter,
over and over, trying to figure out how the company
could justify its position. She had simply asserted her
legal rights, and Whilt was punishing her for that. She
took several deep breaths, trying to calm herself, but
surprisingly, she didn't cry or feel sad. A strange sense of
relief overcame Wanda as she dialed Lambert's number.
The harassment was over. No matter how difficult the
next steps would be, at least she wouldn't be facing Louis
on a daily basis or sitting with the sword of Damocles
over her head.

Lambert advised her in his wise, steady voice, saying
all was on track with the case and this new turn of events
only added fuel to their fire. A second wave of relief
washed over Wanda, but it would be short-lived.

"Ms. Julienne," he continued, "there will be one
other change concerning your case, but it will not impact
the proceedings or outcome in any way. I'm turning your
case over to one of my partners once we receive the trial
date."

"What?" The word came out in a small squeak as
Wanda choked on her own saliva. She started coughing.

"Settle down, Ms. Julienne, everything will be all
right—as long as you are."

"I'm fine," she finally said. "But I don't understand."

"I have to cut back on my time at the firm for
personal reasons. There has been an illness in my family."

"I'm sorry."

"Thank you. For this reason, your case will be better
off in the hands of someone who has the time to
dedicate to it."

"Who will be handling my case?"

"That hasn't yet been decided. But I will keep you

abreast of all developments."

Wanda's heart sank as she hung up the phone.

৵৽

"Wanda! You're supposed to be in bed! What are you and Nelly doing here?" Galina led them into the living room as Wanda unfastened the baby carrier, extricated herself from it and held a sleeping Nelly over one shoulder.

"C'mon, let's set her down in the crib," Galina said.

Moments later, they sat on the couch, gazing out at the Eiffel Tower that no longer represented their virtual meeting point. Then Wanda looked down at her unmanicured nails and the hole in the knee of her jeans. She was not a pretty sight.

"What's happened?" Galina asked.

"I was fired." Her words were barely audible.

"I'm sorry." Galina hugged her, rubbing her greasy hair. Wanda was finally crying, snot dripping out of her nose and onto Galina's designer blouse. But Galina wouldn't care about stained clothing. She held Wanda close until Wanda had cried all of the tears away and sniffled one last time.

"You OK?"

Wanda nodded and settled back against the soft pecan-colored cushions. Then she extricated the letter from her handbag and thrust it toward Galina. At the same time, she explained her lawyer's situation.

"It's a bit much, all at once," Galina said after she finished reading. "As for work, this is a good thing. Shame on them for firing you after you claimed your rights. From a legal standpoint, it was not a judicious move. It could be that your firing is punishment for suing the company. Of course, that must be proven in a courtroom, but that isn't an impossible feat."

Wanda's phone rang. She didn't have to look at it to know who was calling. Max. He'd left messages, and she hadn't returned them. With one hand, she reached into her bag and silenced the phone.

"You can go ahead—" Galina said, raising one perfect eyebrow as she looked over the letter at Wanda.

"No, it's fine."

Galina's eyes studied her, read her, but Galina didn't say another word. Wanda squirmed in her seat, then rose to walk to the bay window.

"Lambert's team will handle this. Now you're free of them." Galina joined her, putting an arm around her shoulders. "It was a matter of time, and I think you understood that."

Wanda nodded. Ever since her return, ever since Elodie's fall, like a terrible omen of what lay ahead, she knew her days at Whilt were numbered. She hadn't allowed herself to believe it. Wanda had been at Whilt for so many years, had felt more than comfortable in her position, knew her clients well enough to ask about their children and grandchildren. And now that part of her life, which often felt like her entire life, had vanished. And that was when the realization hit, crashing down upon her.

Tears shining in her eyes, she turned to Galina.

"Work was the center of your life too," she whispered. "Is this why you walked out?" Galina looked away. Wanda waited, heart pounding. Maybe she was wrong. Maybe she was paranoid, thinking that every woman who went off on maternity leave would return to chaos in the workplace. But the look in her friend's eyes told her she wasn't crazy at all.

"To preclude any problems, I decided to take a few years off," Galina said. "I know how it is at the firm. I understand the demands, and I realized I would be setting myself up for defeat—both personally and professionally—if I returned right away."

Galina's words were calm and steady, as always, but Wanda could sense the underlying tension.

"It wasn't something you necessarily wanted," Wanda murmured.

Galina returned to the couch, poured tea for two and settled back against the cushions. Wanda took a hot cup and sat opposite her friend.

"Sounds awful, doesn't it? That I decided to stay home with my baby to avoid upset in my career—"

"Galina, no, don't say that." Wanda reached out to hold her hand. "You're a wonderful mother!"

Galina smiled. "And I love Anya and love being a mother. But I have to be honest. Professional concerns were part of the picture when I made the decision to take the time off. If they weren't, I probably would have gone to part time for a few years instead. But that was not an option. It's much easier to take a sabbatical and then return as if nothing has changed than wade through those early childhood waters in an environment that isn't sympathetic. Even at the firm, I've seen some rather questionable treatment of women returning from maternity leave."

"Why didn't you tell me?" Wanda asked. But she knew the answer. Wanda was the "problem" friend. Galina was not. Galina's life flowed as smoothly as a river. And if there were any obstacles, she preferred handling them quietly and on her own rather than asking for help.

"So this is why you don't want to go back now. You don't want to dive right in and end up like me."

"I've grown used to the situation," Galina said. "I look at it as a way to spend more time with Anya and preserve my career. And in the end, what's wrong with that?"

"Nothing," Wanda said. "Except that you're not

standing up for much of anything. Instead you're avoiding the problem." Shocked at the disgust she heard in her own voice, Wanda shook her head. "No. Sorry. I shouldn't have said that. You made the smart decision."

Galina smiled. "Don't apologize. I've scolded myself, using words and a tone pretty much like yours, more times than I can count. I'm not proud of my motivations."

"Does Charles know?"

"No."

"Why didn't you deny it when I brought it up just now?"

"Because you were insightful enough to figure it out," Galina said with a sad smile.

Chapter 31

They'd opened a bottle of wine and snacked on cheese and crackers, crumbs littering the usually pristine couch. Galina told Wanda about the pressure and hours at the firm, making the lifestyle incompatible with the first years of motherhood. For the first time ever, her eyes were vulnerable and unsure. The dependable, confident and perfect Galina was human. Wanda, who'd always felt so close to her, now realized there had been something superficial about their relationship. This whole part of her friend's life, and any doubts or concerns of Galina's, had remained hidden from her. Galina hadn't shared of herself; instead, she had been there as an emotional and psychological crutch for Wanda. Everything for Wanda.

Guilt overwhelmed Wanda as she forgot about her own woes and thought of the solitude her friend must have experienced all of these years. Even now, she wouldn't completely break down. It wasn't her nature, and Wanda knew that could never be changed. But why was Galina so guarded?

Wanda took a gulp of wine even though her head

was already spinning from too much of it. Galina refilled both of their glasses and handed Wanda a slice of brie on a hearty cracker "to mop up the alcohol," she said with a smile.

"Galina, why don't you break down like a blubbering fool, like me?" Her speech was slurred, but she didn't care. The question was out, and she wanted an answer. "Why do you hold back?"

Galina took another sip of the wine she managed to hold much better than her friend. She settled back against the cushions, gazed out the window, far beyond Paris, and then turned grave, luminous eyes to Wanda.

"How can I complain when I've always had it so good?" Wanda knew about her upbringing in the lap of luxury, but she didn't know the context.

"My real mother didn't willingly give me up," Galina continued. "She was forced to. I discovered the truth, some letters, when I was sixteen. And by then, my birth mother had passed away, a victim of disease that spread through her small village. This was an ugly, dark secret that weighed on my parents—the people who had raised me. I confronted my father, and he collapsed in tears and told me the whole story. He was elderly by then, as was my mother. I loved them, and they had been desperate to have me. How could I have cast them aside at that point? I did, for a few weeks... I gathered up some belongings and ran away, to the nearest five-star hotel." She smirked and shook her head. "I'd become one of them, Wanda. I'm a fighter in the corporate world, in the world of luxury. I could have bought myself a plane ticket and returned to Nigeria to try to find aunts, cousins. But I didn't. My father tracked me down and when he appeared at the door of my hotel room, I fell into his arms. He told me that he and my mother would support me if I wanted to find this long-lost family. And then I looked up at him, at the golden eyes that were like my own—because, you see, he was my biological father—and I said 'no.'"

Wanda's heart thumped so loudly she felt as if it would pound its way out of her chest. She reached for Galina's hand and squeezed it.

"It's OK," Galina said. "That happened years ago, and I'm at peace with the decision. You know the charitable works I do in some of the Nigerian villages?" Wanda nodded. "That's helped me move forward," Galina continued. "Now, I think of my beginnings any time I might cry or complain, and I think of the new friends I've made there, and I realize I don't have much to gripe about. It's as simple as that."

She shrugged and smiled, the usual confidence slowly but surely returning.

"You must think I'm such a wimp," Wanda mumbled, sinking deeper into the cushion and pulling a matching blanket up to her chin.

"Of course not! Our personal experiences affect the way we handle events in our lives. Period."

Wanda thought of her own rather boring middle class upbringing in the two-family house on a tree-lined street. There hadn't been any exciting family secrets or adventures. She hadn't been raised to confront corporate giants or unfairness in the workplace. She hadn't been raised with tools to fight injustice. Wanda had been raised as someone who believed that hard work resulted in appreciation and a decent level of success. *Naïve fool*, she thought.

Galina stood up, breaking into Wanda's reverie, and took her by the hand. "C'mon, I think you're going to be spending the night in the guest room."

Chapter 32

Two month's pay and then unemployment benefits. But unemployment would be even more meager than her new salary. Wanda squinted over a spreadsheet of her own finances. There were many columns for expenses—rent, food, electricity, water, baby supplies—and only one with her pitiful revenue. At the end of a month, she would be in the red if she didn't adjust the costs she could control. She refused to ask her parents for assistance. She was beyond that at her age. Depending on them all over again would feel like defeat, as if she had accomplished nothing. Max had sent a check in the mail with a note begging her to accept it. She hadn't ripped it up, but she hadn't cashed it either.

Why are you refusing his help? she asked herself. As Nelly's father, it was only fair that he split the costs of raising her. Yet something held Wanda back. Deep inside, she feared it would become a simple business arrangement, an obligation, and somehow, any feelings he had for her would soon disappear. Deliriously, she dreamed he would keep his distance and then return when she was ready, when the situation with Whilt was far behind her.

Wanda blinked, her eyes now bleary from staring at the computer screen, and walked to the skylight. She pulled it open and stood on a stepstool to look out at the grimy street below and the passersby heading to work or school. If only she was still one of those women in silky skirts and high heels, one of those people with bags digging into their shoulders and telephones at their ears. The noise of the avenue rose to her ears—the honking of horns, the yelling, the laughter—and the scent of diesel filled her nose. Nothing like her old neighborhood where everything was calmer, cleaner. She leaned on her elbows and studied the sight for a while, letting herself be hypnotized by it until the ringing of her phone snapped her back to the present.

She hopped off the stool and answered before the call went to voicemail.

It was Maddie. "I know you lost your job. I'm sorry, Wanda. I only found out this morning. And I'm sorry I couldn't help you earlier, to avoid this."

Wanda sighed. "It couldn't have been avoided. How could I be angry with you when you're just trying to keep your job too? And it's none of my business why you want to stay at that place. I was being unreasonable and desperate. And that was ridiculous, because no matter what, they were going to fire me."

"It's all right." Her voice was soothing, kind, as it had always been. "How about meeting me for lunch? Please. It's my treat. I'd like to speak with you about something."

Wanda hesitated as she glanced at Nelly, calmly playing on her activity mat. She had taken up enough of Galina's time over the past few days. And after the middle-of-the-night conversation they'd shared, maybe Galina needed some time alone with her thoughts. She wasn't around simply to serve as Wanda's sounding board. And Wanda certainly didn't have the budget for the nanny, who had tears in her eyes when Wanda had explained the situation. Now, it would only be reasonable to hire her for a few hours here or there when Wanda had a job interview.

"I'm with Nelly, I don't know—"

"That's fine, Wanda. Bring her along. I've been there, you know."

Traipsing across town with Nelly in the carrier wasn't fun, especially considering the baby's weight at eight months old, but Wanda didn't like how she'd left off with Maddie. She regretted her words and wanted a chance to patch things up. And apparently Maddie had something to tell her.

Wanda promised to meet Maddie at noon and then hurried through the tasks she'd put off since she'd stuck her nose in the computer. She threw on a pair of jeans, but paired them with red ballerina flats and a matching oxford shirt instead of the beat-up sneakers and old turtlenecks she'd been wearing lately. A light jacket and she was ready to go.

But as Wanda slipped out the door with Nelly at her chest, she almost tripped on a massive box with a bow on top. Her name was written in big letters, but she didn't recognize the handwriting. This was obviously from Max or Galina, but nowhere could she find a clue. She ripped at the paper and drew in a sharp breath when she saw this was a gift she couldn't refuse: a stroller.

Before leaving, Wanda sent text messages to Galina and Max, asking if either of them had left the gift at her door. She didn't receive a reply.

◈

March in Paris could either be an extension of winter, or a beacon signaling the warmth and sunshine to come. On this particular day, the breeze was gentle, an early taste of spring, as it tossed Wanda's hair back from her face. Effortlessly, she wheeled Nelly along the wide sidewalks of the sixteenth arrondissement, flanked by plane trees changing their look from gray to green. The sixteenth had plenty of busy avenues and tourist attractions, but there were even more tranquil residential areas that transported Wanda far from city life. As she walked, she savored this sense of calm.

She met Maddie at the café where they used to have lunch. For the quiche/salad combo they ordered each time. But today, after so many days of reheated noodles and other uninteresting dinners, the salad had never seemed so crisp, the quiche never so tender and fragrant.

Maddie and Wanda chatted about this and that for a few minutes, as if neither wanted to broach painful subjects. Wanda appreciated this seat at the back of the terrace, tucked between overflowing planters and the glass window. It was quiet so Nelly could snooze and they could talk without overhearing and being overheard by the businesspeople making deals over wine at the tables closest to the street.

Wanda remembered those days, the long business lunches over several courses and lots of wine. Everything had tasted pretty much the same as she focused on the numbers in her spreadsheets instead of the flavors on her plate. And how much waste was Whilt money responsible for? She hated to think of the quantity of champagne, *foie gras*, truffles and other delicacies that ended up in the trash.

When they finished the last bits of lettuce and ordered two coffees, Maddie took a deep breath and lowered her voice.

"You're not the only one leaving Whilt," she said.

"They're doing this to someone else?" Wanda's hands gripped the water glass so tightly she nearly broke it.

"I'm leaving, and with an… agreement."

"But you wanted to stay." Wanda thought back to their last conversation and the weariness on Maddie's face. "I didn't understand why, but I knew you wanted to stay. And I'm sorry. It was none of my business. I shouldn't have gotten angry with you."

"You don't have to apologize again. I understood your frustration. You see, I never wanted to hang onto that job—I needed to. But things have evolved."

Maddie's blue eyes caught hers, and all of a sudden, Wanda realized there was more to be told, and Maddie was about to tell it.

"Wanda, I didn't sign the financial disclosure agreement. I couldn't. If I did, they would have learned that my finances were a disaster and that I desperately needed to keep my job. I would have lost all leverage. They would have demoted me."

"But you have dirt on Louis!"

"Well, so do you…"

"I… I guess I do, but I'm not as high up in the Whilt food chain."

Maddie smirked. "Yes, you're right. What I had to say would carry more weight than what you might say. But I knew that wouldn't last very long. Once Whilt saw the debts, they would do a bit more digging, and they would discover Henri's alcoholism, the gambling. If I dared to drag Louis and the company through the mud, they would ruin Henri's name and my name forever."

"Oh Maddie, I'm sorry, I had no idea."

"No one does. Even close friends don't realize what's happened over the past five years. It started when he was ousted from the firm. He couldn't get back on his feet, the cocktail hours extended into days. And that's how the story goes."

Wanda held her head in her hands as the waiter set two cups of coffee before them. She inhaled the bittersweet scent, usually one of her favorites, but today it nearly made her gag.

"So I preempted the drama. I offered Whilt the opportunity to settle with me unless the company wanted me to speak with the press. This isn't just about Louis. They don't care about him or anyone else. If it was about him, they would have let him fall and saved some money. No, this is about the Whilt culture. And that, they will defend to the death."

"And you agreed to never divulge what you know." Wanda tried to hide the disappointment in her voice. Before, there was hope that maybe, just maybe, Maddie would change her mind and help Wanda gather a bit of evidence or provide an affidavit. But now, all was lost.

Wanda sipped her drink, burning her palate, and winced. Tears rose into her eyes, but she blinked them back.

"Why are you telling me this?" she asked.

"Because I wanted you to know that a court subpoena overrides any nondisclosure agreement I may sign."

Wanda knitted her eyebrows. "You would—"

"I wouldn't have a choice," Maddie said.

"Maddie, I never thought... I figured Whilt employees would lie in this sort of situation, too afraid of losing their jobs."

"How right you are."

Now Wanda smiled, a wan little smile, but a smile nonetheless, as she thanked Maddie. She had faith in this woman, who if called to testify, would do so truthfully. Wanda wasn't foolish enough to think Maddie's allegiance would change the outcome of her case, but perhaps this ally—this possibility—was one bright spot at the end of a long, dark tunnel.

Chapter 33

The screen of Wanda's cell phone lit up as she huddled in the corner of her bed, a book against her knees. It was past midnight, and she couldn't sleep. She'd fallen into a rhythm of insomnia, unbroken by warm milk or the music of crashing waves. She tried counting stars and sheep, and watching movies. And then she decided to accept it, reading into the wee hours and then the next day forgetting exactly when her eyes had slipped from the page.

Wanda's phone shouldn't have been on. Usually she turned it off much earlier than this. Her shoulders stiffened, sending her book to the floor with a thud, as the text message arrived.

Yes, I brought the stroller by.

Max. He must have just finished his shift at the hospital.

Wanda typed and retyped several times, words she meant but wasn't ready to say: *I'm sorry, I love you, come over, I want you here with me.* Then she erased them all and simply wrote: *Thank you.*

She tossed the phone back onto the bed, pretending

she didn't care if he replied when really that was all she cared about right in that instant.

A few minutes passed. *Give up, turn off that thing*, she told herself. And then it buzzed.

Max: *How are you?*

Wanda: *OK. You?*

Max: *Tired.*

She held her breath. He could have said "pissed off at you for pushing me away," but he didn't. She could have turned off her phone, angry that he had walked out on her and called her selfish. But she didn't. Max was right. She had been thinking of her own pride before anything else. Still, even knowing this, Wanda was scared to take the risk of being hurt. Whilt had left her broken. She needed time alone to rebuild her confidence, her faith in the world and the people around her.

Max: *Finally having dinner. Reheated takeout noodles. You'd love it.*

Wanda smiled, then typed: *Same dinner here.*

Max: *Under the same stars.*

Wanda: *Yes.*

She pictured those stars from the window of his apartment as they lay side by side, tracing constellations with their fingers. She wanted to be there, back in that moment.

Max: *So when can I see you?*

Wanda took a breath and answered before her heart could instruct her otherwise: *I need some time.*

Max: *You want to see how long I'll hold on before giving up?*

Wanda: *You're probably about to.*

Max: *Give up?*

Wanda: *Yeah.*

Wanda bit her lip. She was being unreasonable. How long would be long enough? When would she trust him? When would she truly believe he wanted to be with her and wasn't sticking with her because he felt trapped?

After the trial, she told herself, but she had no reason—scientific or sentimental—to back that up.

The phone buzzed.

I don't give up this easily.

Wanda read the words over and over. She was about to continue the conversation, then changed her mind and typed: *It's late, Max.*

Max: *Why aren't you sleeping?*

Wanda: *Insomnia.*

Max: *Well, that's obvious but...*

Wanda: *Boredom, maybe. I miss my job, and job prospects are abysmal.*

Max: *Wouldn't it be better if we were together?*

Of course it would. But Wanda couldn't give herself that gift right now. She studied the phone for a few minutes and almost thought it would vibrate once again, but it didn't.

So she typed: *Goodnight, Max.*

He didn't reply.

Chapter 34

The job interviews were almost nonexistent. The job listings were almost nonexistent. So when Wanda was called for a fund management position at a firm in the old neighborhood, tears flooded her eyes. After weeks of searching, weeks of believing there wasn't a single position in her field in that city...

For the first time in a long while, she tossed aside her jeans and donned a real, professional outfit. She looked at her reflection in the mirror and swallowed hard. The same beige silk dress she had worn many times to work, along with the matching suede heels. The smooth ponytail and tasteful nude makeup. She should have looked the same as she did during her days back at Whilt, yet somehow she didn't. There was a change in her face that she couldn't identify. A sense of melancholy even when she forced a smile.

She stared at herself for a while, as if observing a stranger—a pathetic stranger. The nanny's voice from the other side of the dressing screen broke Wanda from her thoughts. Colette would take Nelly for a walk in the park, then put her down for a nap if she hadn't already fallen asleep.

"Sure, that's fine," Wanda called out. Colette carried the baby over for a quick goodbye, and then the door closed behind their soft voices.

Confidence, confidence, Wanda repeated to herself as she grabbed her handbag, avoided the mirror and set off for her interview.

৩~৶

In the half hour she waited in the conference room, Wanda chewed down one nail, checked her cell phone a dozen times and filled the margins of two pages of her notebook with calculations pertaining to her personal finances. She glanced up a few times at the boring white walls bearing modern art in shades of black and gray.

"Wanda Julienne? Hello, I'm Joyce Cooper." A woman about Wanda's age entered and shook her hand. Her glossy dark hair was wound into a thick bun at the top of her head, and she wore a bright purple dress—an appearance that made her stand out against the blandness of the office. Her smile was wide and bright, but her eyes looked wistful.

She and Wanda sat, and Wanda didn't have to wait long to understand the wistfulness.

"I'm sorry, but I have to be honest: We're wasting your time. You're well overqualified for the position we have to offer."

Wanda's heart sank.

"My assistant shouldn't have called you in for an interview. I just found out an hour ago, too late to cancel. There might have been some confusion between candidates since we received so much interest in this position."

"I'm still interested, Ms. Cooper." Wanda's voice took on a pleading tone that shamed her, but she set aside her pride and instead thought about the bills she had to pay. "I don't expect to find a position identical to the one I'd had at Whilt."

"Ms. Julienne, believe me, you wouldn't last longer than a day in this job. You're well beyond it. I had a look at your resume and your fund performance. You're an excellent catch for any firm. You would leave us as soon as the opportunity arose. This job pays less than half of what you made at Whilt."

"But would you hire me if I was all right with that?"

"No," she said flatly. "We have plenty of candidates perfectly suited to the job. It wouldn't make strategic sense for us to under-employ and then lose that employee when they found a better opportunity. And don't say that won't happen. Because it will. I've experienced it and don't want to again."

Her voice was pleasant but firm. Wanda sighed.

"Look, I know it's difficult out there." Ms. Cooper's sharp dark eyes held Wanda's. "Senior positions are scarce. I'm hoping things will turn around. But if they don't, you would be better off changing careers than settling for a job so far below your level. When that happens, everyone is miserable, and performance suffers."

Ms. Cooper was right, but Wanda couldn't overcome the disappointment rising within. She forced herself to smile, to make small talk as the woman escorted her down the hall. And then she was alone, walking along the vast tree-lined avenue on this perfect spring day. She remembered the days spent ensconced behind her desk at Whilt. She remembered longing for the outdoors, for the gentle breeze on her cheek, for the scent of flowers in the air. And now, all she wished for were four walls, a computer and a paycheck.

Chapter 35

The man on the other end of the line told Wanda his name was Michael Smith and he was a reporter for *The Times*. A strange feeling of nausea rose from the pit of her stomach. She had been curled up in the corner of the couch with her laptop, scrolling through the job listings as raindrops pelted the windows above. Every once in a while, she leaned over the edge to rock the lounger where Nelly napped. The ring of her phone had cut through this calm picture, jarring Wanda so that she almost dropped her computer. Now, she stood at the window near the kitchen sink, gazing at the grayness beyond and waiting for Michael Smith to confirm her suspicions.

"We hear you're suing your former employer, Whilt, and we'd like to hear your story," he said.

Suspicion confirmed.

"Where did you get your information?" she asked. "And how did you find my phone number?"

"An anonymous tip. Sorry, I can't reveal sources."

Wanda's mind raced through the possibilities: Anyone in Whilt upper management, Louis, Maddie, Max, Galina. Clearly, it wasn't in Whilt's interest to make a lot of noise about the case so they were off the list. That left the people who were closest to her. Except for her parents, who didn't know she no longer worked at Whilt. She hadn't told them, hoping she could cover things up until she found a new job.

But Wanda didn't have time to further analyze the situation. Michael Smith cleared his throat and continued, "So how about a phone chat, Ms. Julienne? We could do it at a time that suits you. We'd like to hear your side."

"My side? Do you plan on publishing something whether I talk with you or not?" Her hand was gripping the phone so tightly that her knuckles turned white. She winced, switched hands, and leaned against the counter as if without it for support, she would collapse.

"I can't answer that."

"Why are you doing this?" Wanda's voice came out like a growl.

"It's of interest to a lot of our readers."

"If this is true, and I am suing Whilt, what would your readers care about one person's fight against her employer?"

"It's human interest. It's something a lot of people can relate to."

Yeah, human interest all right, she thought. *You mean "fodder for people's curiosity."* If she was famous, the tabloids would be calling right now offering her cash for a few quotes. The whole idea made Wanda sick. Whether a paper had money to offer her or not, she refused to step into a grotesque version of the limelight. She didn't want to speak to anyone except the lawyers and the judge about what had happened at Whilt.

"I decline to comment on anything at this time," Wanda said, borrowing words she'd read many times before. That would put a stop to this pesky reporter. He didn't have a story without her comments.

"Think about it," he said. "You don't have to decide

on the spot. Here's my contact information…"

And as he rattled it off, Wanda—determined to never speak with him again—still took note.

∽◈∾

Calls and emails from the press multiplied. Within days, Wanda had fended off various attempts to break down her resolve and spill her story. Her insomnia worsened, putting her on a schedule much like that of Nelly, napping throughout the day after a sleepless night. And it was during those nights that Wanda tossed and turned, trying to figure out who had contacted the press. Who would admit to such a thing? Maddie and Max each vehemently denied it.

And deep down, she knew they hadn't been the ones to call the journalists with this scoop. Maddie was involved in her own settlement with Whilt. She wouldn't take the risk. Max wasn't involved enough in the story to take that sort of initiative.

Wanda hadn't called Galina. She told herself Galina wouldn't do it, wouldn't interfere, but the more she thought about it, the more she realized she was lying to herself. Right from the start, Galina was all about taking action. Was this the type of action she was now taking, and if so, why?

Chapter 36

The ringing of Wanda's phone woke her from a midafternoon nap. Seeing her mother's name through bleary eyes, she answered, her voice nothing more than a croak. Nelly snoozed peacefully in her crib as Wanda slipped off the bed, and phone at her ear, settled in the farthest possible point in the apartment: the bathroom.

"Wanda Julienne, what exactly is going on?"

"What are you talking about?" Wanda sat on the toilet lid and thanked God her mother couldn't see how awful she looked: greasy hair, oversized sweatshirt and holey boxer shorts. *A real picture of success*, she thought.

"Well, I was reading *The Times,* and I learned that my daughter was fired from Whilt," she said, her voice trembling. "Wanda, how could you keep this from me?"

Wanda's heart flip flopped. He did it. That goddamned reporter had found a way to write about her. But she couldn't sit here cursing him or even reverse the damage. She had a panicking mother on the line.

"Mom, I'm OK. I've got enough money to live on, and job prospects look good—"

"You're lying. I know you live right up to your last

dime, and I know the economy is terrible. Why didn't you tell me what was going on? What's wrong with you, Wanda?"

"Look, I didn't want to worry you. And what do you know about my finances?"

She was insulted by her mother's comment even though it was true.

"Your father and I are going to wire you some money—"

"No. I'm fine. I've got unemployment and some savings, and Max is helping out."

"I'm disappointed you didn't share this with us, Wanda. Haven't I always kept that door open—"

"Mom, please." Wanda sighed as noisily as possible.

"Will you tell me if you need something, Wanda? That's the problem. You and Nelly could be living on the street, and I wouldn't know until it was in the newspaper!"

"Let's not be dramatic, Mom."

"I love you, Wanda, and I'm worried. That's all."

"I'm sorry. I know."

"And the harassment. Did anyone ever—"

"It didn't get far, Mom," Wanda said, discomfort in her voice.

Now it was her mother's turn to sigh.

"Listen, I need some time to work things out. I didn't even know that stupid reporter was running a story." Wanda ran her hand through her hair, pulling strands from her disheveled ponytail. "I've got to get going. Nelly's going to be up soon."

"Will you—" her mother began.

"I'll keep you posted."

It was obvious that neither mother nor daughter believed those words.

Wanda switched on her computer and sat at the kitchen counter as she searched for her name and Whilt.

The Times wasn't the only one with a story. The world wasn't necessarily interested in Wanda Julienne, but the world was interested in Whilt—especially Whilt behaving badly.

The papers reported Wanda Julienne had filed suit against the company, according to public documents. Unnamed sources cited discrimination and sexual harassment as reasons for the suit. *The Times'* story went on to say that Whilt had been plagued with troubles in the past year, beginning with the accidental death of Elodie Clark, who had fallen to her death from a conference room window. Wanda shuddered. That case had been closed before it was even opened.

Wanda wondered how her case could garner more attention from the press than a story as tragic as Elodie's. The person who spilled her story obviously knew it would spark interest or else he or she wouldn't have gone to the trouble of spilling it. And it was at that second that she was certain about the identity of the source.

She had to see Galina. Her friend had done this, had contacted reporters. She wanted Wanda's name out there. But why? She certainly had a plan. That was how Galina operated.

ふ⁓

They met at a café neither of them had ever been to, in a neighborhood halfway between their apartments. A neutral spot for a conversation Wanda expected to be emotional. They were the only ones on the terrace, under the heat lamps, on this damp afternoon.

They ordered coffee, and Galina asked for two slices of chocolate tart.

"But I—"

"My treat. You're losing weight. Don't tell me you're not because I can see it."

Wanda shrugged. "I don't know. I never weigh myself."

"Well, you should."

"At the moment, I've been too busy fending off the press." Wanda stared into Galina's dark eyes even though she knew her friend wouldn't flinch. The vulnerability she glimpsed during their last encounter had vanished behind the cool façade.

"Yes, I contacted a few news organizations," Galina said.

"Damn it, Galina!" Wanda hissed. "Why? I thought, especially after our last conversation, that you understood how difficult this was for me! Why would you drag this out in the public?"

The waiter set down their coffee and desserts, and Galina took a spoonful of tart and chewed thoughtfully.

"It wasn't arbitrary, Wanda. And it wasn't intended to hurt you. I did it because it's time for you to step forward."

"What do you mean? This is a private matter!" Wanda's voice bordered on hysteria. She didn't want attention—from the media or anyone else. She wanted justice and a new job.

"Wanda, this isn't about you alone. This is about what companies are doing to women and to experienced employees. You aren't the only one who has been forced out for having a baby or making too much money."

"So you want me to be the poster child for the cause? Thanks, Galina. Why didn't you tell reporters that you left your job before this could happen to you?"

Galina winced at the harshness of the words. Wanda was angrier at her friend than she had ever been before. For years, the control Galina had exerted over her life had been comforting, but today, it was suffocating.

"I don't have a story to tell, Wanda," she said. "I didn't stand up to anyone. I turned away. You stood up."

Wanda softened for an instant at the sadness she saw in her friend's eyes but not enough to back down and forgive her on the spot. Galina's weakness didn't give her the right to push her friend's private case into the public eye.

"This is about making the case known," Galina continued, "with the hope that others who have experienced the same treatment at the hand of Whilt will come forward."

"To testify on my behalf?"

"Perhaps."

Wanda studied Galina, who managed to eat her dessert in spite of the tension that reigned. Wanda hadn't touched her plate, hadn't sipped her coffee. Wanda was in turmoil, while Galina remained calm. As usual. Wanda held her head in her hands.

"What is it, Wanda?"

"Why didn't you ask me first?"

"Because you would have refused."

"And you know best."

"I'm not saying I know what's best in every situation. But in this one, I do. I represented companies, I saw what they did to their employees, Wanda. I understand how bad it can get. I know your enemy."

Wanda sighed. "I don't understand you. You don't want to take my case, yet you're in the background pulling strings. Technically, you could handle my case without going back to the firm. We both know that. And you don't tell me what you're doing behind my back because you don't trust my ability to make a good decision."

"That's ridiculous. First of all, it's not as easy as you think to pick up your case and handle it. I'm used to the structure of the firm. Secondly—and this is very important—I trust you, but you're in foreign waters here. I'm doing what I can to help—"

"On your terms. Well, I'm tired of your terms, Galina. I'm tired of you taking control at will and then expecting me to accept it with a smile. I'm tired of the fact that you don't take my suggestions seriously, yet I have to accept everything you say because you've always been the smartest, most successful one. I'm just tired."

Wanda pushed her plate away, grabbed her jacket and the stroller, and hurried away before Galina—even Galina, who always had the perfect answer—could respond.

Chapter 37

Wanda spent the next twenty-four hours in bed, only rising to take care of Nelly. She slept odd hours and the rest of the time monitored newspapers and websites. One of the most gossipy sites—one that had harassed her with more than a few calls—reported that Louis was cited in more than one case against Whilt. As long as the papers didn't say much about her, Wanda didn't care what they reported about the company.

She tried to distract herself with books, but each time, she had to reread the same paragraph over and over. She couldn't concentrate. Thoughts of Whilt and the trial were ever present in her mind even though she hadn't heard a word from anyone at the company, and Lambert had told her that the case was in the attorneys' hands—not hers. She needed to get on with her life. But how?

Wanda let messages pile up from reporters, her mother, Max and Galina. She only answered a call from Lambert.

"We have the date," he announced, sending her heartbeat into a frenzy. "November second."

"November? That's seven months from now!" She bolted out of bed and padded barefoot across the rough wooden floor. She took a sip of the orange juice she'd poured into a glass hours ago. It was warm and bitter.

"I told you we would have to be patient."

"I know… I just thought it would be a couple of months."

"Based on?"

"Nothing. Based on my own wishful thinking." She made her way back to bed and settled down with a thump.

"This is actually good news, Ms. Julienne. The wait could have extended into next year."

"You're right. I need to put things into perspective." Wanda pulled the comforter up to her chin and leaned back against the wall. Raindrops pattered onto the window above. More April showers.

"What about the future of my case?" she continued. "When are you handing it over, and who will be taking it on?"

"I have to wrap up a few final details so I'll hold onto it for the next two weeks, at which point I will hand it over to the very competent Constance Dupuis."

Wanda had no preconceived idea about the competence of Constance Dupuis or anyone else at the firm, but she still didn't relish changing the status quo. In any case, she didn't have a choice in the matter.

Chapter 38

Wanda cashed Max's check. She had budgeted her money carefully but hadn't counted on her laptop conking out. She'd spent half the day on the line with technical assistance, and the consensus was simple: She needed a new computer. Wanda considered doing without, then realized she wouldn't have much luck in her job hunt without one. So she ordered a new machine online, set for delivery in forty-eight hours, and texted Max a thank you along with an explanation.

I'll pay you back, she wrote.

He didn't reply. Another check showed up in the mail the next day.

Wanda set the envelope on the counter and retreated to the bathroom, where she looked at herself in the mirror. It was a weekly routine that allowed her to monitor her own deterioration. The greasy hair, dark circles under eyes, holey sweatpants and stained tank top. She was a complete mess. She peeled off her clothes, stepped into the shower and turned on the blast of warm water as if it would remove all that had been destroying her.

Wanda pulled an oversized green tunic over her head to disguise her more-boyish-than-ever figure and worked wonders on her face with a concealer stick. She took a step back and again looked into that mirror. *Mirror, mirror on the wall, who is the most disguised of all?* She smirked as she said the words to herself. No one would guess she was the same woman who had run down to the mailboxes an hour ago.

She told herself she would take this little outing to assure Max that she and Nelly were doing just fine and not in need of his help—but deep down, she knew it was an excuse to see him.

Wanda had called the hospital to find out if he was working that day. She avoided the emotional disorder a trip to his apartment might bring. At ten minutes to six, she lingered in front of the automatic doors, watching the change of shifts. Nurses and doctors flooding in and out. Visitors—some happy, some distraught—milling around with cell phones to their ears. And a few patients wheeling IV bags at their sides on a quest for a bit of fresh air. The rain that had fallen earlier in the day had transformed into a gentle mist that didn't even warrant an umbrella.

Wanda's heart fluttered as she saw Max, chatting with a few colleagues. When he turned, his eyes locked with hers, and they both moved in each other's direction until they met. He knelt down to greet Nelly and scooped her into his arms. She smiled and started warbling in her own little language, clearly happy to see him.

"To what do I owe this lovely visit?"

Wanda hesitated, her gaze meeting the tips of her damp ballerina flats.

"I wanted to let you know that we're OK and really

the check I cashed was an exception, an emergency situation," she mumbled, her words falling over each other. "You should stop sending those checks, Max. We're fine."

"This time it came in handy. Another time it might as well. Use the money when you need it, as you need it."

"I didn't come here to have the same conversation we already had," she said, willing her voice not to sound whiny. "I don't want to be your charity case."

Max's phone rang. "Excuse me," he said to Wanda before greeting whoever was on the line. Wanda's eyes returned to her shoes again, to the beige patent leather and the green cord forming a bow over the toes. A gift from Galina, tailor-made for her. Her whole life seemed to be defined by Galina.

"Yeah, I'm going to be about a half hour late. Just pick any place you'd like to go. I'm fine with it."

Wanda's ears pricked up. Max had a date. This wasn't just a get-together with a friend. She could feel it. Wanda tried to squelch feelings of jealousy, tried to hide the scarlet color of her cheeks by letting her hair drape over them.

When Max hung up, she held out her hands for Nelly.

"It's time for us to go," she said. "We don't want to interrupt your evening." She sounded petulant, and she could have kicked herself for it, for showing she cared.

"You're not interrupting anything, Wanda." He kissed Nelly on the head before handing her over.

"Well, you obviously have plans."

"The plans can wait."

"It's a shame to be late on my account when you could be enjoying a—" Wanda was getting herself in deeper and deeper. She should have changed the subject rather than pathetically forcing him to tell her that, yes, he had put thoughts of her behind him, and yes, he was going on a date.

"It's not exactly a date."

"You can go on a date if you'd like, Max. We're not married or anything." She finished strapping Nelly into the stroller and then stood up to face Max, who now placed his hands on her shoulders and drew her closer.

"Why do you keep fighting us, Wanda?" His breath was warm against her cheek. His soapy scent was overpowered by the smell of hospital cleaning products, a fragrance he washed away with a hot shower as soon as he set foot in his apartment. Wanda had grown used to the routine. Then that soapy scent would return.

"You're the one who has a date, Max." She took a step back.

He laughed ironically and shook his head. "I'm having a casual dinner with a fellow doctor. We're friends. I don't plan on it developing into something more. I would rather develop something more with you, but you keep turning your back on the possibility."

Everything he said was true, yet she was too stubborn to admit it, to swallow her pride and take the complicated road of pursuing a new relationship.

"I've got to go," she said. "Have fun tonight."

"Wanda…" He took her hand, but she pushed him away. "You can't tell me you came here just to say 'stop sending money.'"

And once again, he was right.

Chapter 39

Another rainy spring day and Wanda sat on her bed, in her ratty sweatpants, munching on pretzels and scrolling through job listings. It was a depressing routine. There wasn't much out there. And when there was something, even a position that matched her experience to perfection, she didn't get called in for an interview. Yet, she continued searching each day, sending out resumes, monitoring the stock market and reading about the best-performing companies in order to keep her feet wet in the business. And of course reading about herself now and then as rumors surrounding Whilt escalated. Although she had been upset by the media coverage at the start, she now felt indifferent. She didn't care what the newspapers and online media had to say. The only thing that was important was the judge's decision.

Wanda's phone rang—a number she didn't recognize—and she answered mid-chew.

"Wanda? This is Kate Mancini."

Kate! From Whilt. The Kate who was suing Whilt, who hadn't responded to her messages. Wanda's heart raced, and she reached for water to wash down the bit of pretzel sticking in her throat.

"Yes, hi, I'm glad you called."

"You probably thought I never would. Things have been difficult. Anyway, can we meet? The baby is due in two months, and I'm on bed rest. Maybe you can stop by my place?"

That was it. A brief phone call, no explanation, no small talk. Wanda agreed to visit Kate that afternoon.

℥

Wanda had been to Kate's palatial apartment once before. A Christmas party. She still remembered the massive tree in the living room, its bulbs twinkling against the backdrop of city lights and the elegant chandeliers dipping low over coffee tables. Kate lived on the Boulevard Saint-Germain, a long avenue known for its cafés and artistic atmosphere. Kate's husband was a writer, but their wealth didn't come from his works of literary fiction. It came from Kate's trust fund. Her father had been an oil magnate in Texas. Kate could have basked in this life of luxury without lifting a finger, but she didn't. She chose to work hard at Whilt, bending to the company's demands and trying to climb the corporate ladder.

Kate had always been quiet about her family fortune, but secrets were not easily kept at Whilt. She'd been there only a few months when word began to leak out. Kate's maiden name was Holden, like John Edward Holden III of the oil fortune. From that moment forward, she had been the subject of gossip, with the others asking why on earth she was wasting her time at Whilt when she could be on a beach somewhere basking in the sun. Wanda had never had that attitude regarding Kate. She respected the fact that Kate wanted to build her own career and enjoyed her work.

The doors of the roomy glass elevator opened, and Wanda was grateful; she wouldn't have to maneuver Nelly and the stroller up any stairs, like she often had to in other Parisian buildings. Nelly had dozed off on the brisk walk from the subway station to the apartment, and Wanda didn't want to disturb her.

Kate greeted them, looking her elegant self in spite of obvious fatigue. Her long blond hair draped over one shoulder of an airy peach-colored dress that swept the glossy hardwood floor. She kissed Wanda on both cheeks, oohed and ahhed over Nelly, and led them into the living room that Wanda remembered from the party. Works of Chagall and Picasso were new additions to the walls. Perhaps inherited when Kate's father passed away a year earlier.

"Please have a seat." She held her back with one hand and gestured toward an ivory love seat with another. She lay on a matching sofa. "You'll have to excuse me."

"Of course, I understand."

"The doctor says I should be horizontal as much as possible. Otherwise, life is about the same as usual." A smile lit up her face.

They chatted for a few minutes about pregnancy, babies and the like. Kate said her two older children were in the nursery down the hall with the nanny, and if Nelly awoke, she could join them. A housekeeper hurried in with a silver tray of coffee and tea, and upon Kate's request, poured them cups of tea.

"Hope that's all right?" she said suddenly. "I remember seeing you sip tea a lot at the office."

"You're observant," Wanda said, accepting the cup. "Thank you, that's perfect."

"When you called and left a message, there was a reason I didn't reply right away," Kate began. "As you know, I filed a lawsuit against Whilt. But I wasn't sure where I was going with everything. My pregnancy has been tough… so I wondered if I even had the energy to go through with a case against the company. I was close to turning around and forgetting about it. My attorney urged me on though. You see, Whilt has set a precedent of buying out desperate ex-employees left and right, for sums smaller than they would get if they took things through the proper legal channels."

She paused and took a sip of tea.

"Most of these former Whilt employees take the cash because they can't afford to wait months and even years for a court decision. I'm different. I can afford to wait. I don't need Whilt's money. I'm not doing any of this for money. I'm doing this for justice."

She smiled again, more brilliantly than before, as Wanda stared, wide-eyed, and sipped her Earl Grey. Kate was exactly the kind of employee Whilt despised: one who couldn't be bought.

"So you will go through with the lawsuit?" Wanda asked.

"Yes. It's my duty to go through with it. For those who've suffered the same sort of treatment but couldn't stand up and fight." Kate's voice was firm. "And that is why I contacted you. Now that I'm sure about continuing my case, I'd like to put our attorneys in touch. I think we could help each other."

Now Wanda was the one smiling. Kate had thrown her a lifeline, and she would accept it.

❧

Kate said her troubles with Whilt began after she had her second child and aimed for a promotion to senior fund manager.

"When I didn't have kids, I spent most of my time in the office—beyond required hours—and didn't cost the company much. The economy was going strong, and I'd had a couple of good raises that were fine at first. But I'm sure Whilt regretted them later."

"Yeah, when the company started hiring younger, cheaper labor, and the economy took a nosedive," Wanda snapped.

"Exactly. That all happened around the time my second baby was born. I got back from maternity leave, looking forward to applying again for a senior fund manager position. Louis refused, saying I had been gone for 'so long' that it wasn't possible to evaluate whether or not I would do well in the job. Bullshit, of course. The only thing that had changed was I'd had a baby. I hadn't delivered my brain along with the baby. Then came the mediocre performance evaluation, built on nothing—comparisons with others managing different sorts of funds in other regions."

Goose bumps rose along Wanda's arms as Kate spoke. This was her story. With a few new details for variety. But the pattern remained the same. How many other women had experienced it too? At Whilt and elsewhere?

"Things reached an all-time low a few months ago, when Louis suggested I have an abortion."

"They suggested that to me too." Wanda's breath caught in her throat for a moment. "They gave me an address."

Kate squeezed her eyes shut and shook her head.

"Over and over," she said. "How many women take them up on this? How many, desperate for their jobs, give in to the pressure? A company—a job—has no place dictating whether a woman should or shouldn't carry a baby to term."

They were both silent for a few minutes, and then Kate sighed and continued her story. Her eyes wandered out the window, to the trees sporting their new green coats and the balconies lining ornate, historic buildings across the avenue.

"Then the sexual harassment began. I say it 'began,' but Louis had made inappropriate comments before. At this point, let's say he became bolder."

She told Wanda of his remarks about her "ass" or clothing, of his attempts to lure her to a bar, of his threats concerning her job.

"And the grand finale?" Kate said, sarcasm in her voice. "Whilt fired me for insubordination. They fired me for fighting back. Now tell me your story."

Wanda took a deep breath and studied Kate's sharp determined eyes. This was a woman she could trust.

"It's the mirror image of yours."

Chapter 40

The sun had set by the time Wanda left Kate's apartment. She ambled down the street, her silhouette casting night shadows along the sidewalk. Kate's story, and the idea of collaboration, filled her with a fresh sense of purpose and renewed her energy. This wasn't one small case, all about Wanda Julienne. It was much larger than that. It was a real issue, affecting women not only at Whilt, but at other companies. She wasn't counting on her case, or even a handful of cases, eliminating the problem from the face of the earth. But maybe if she fought to the best of her ability, if Kate did the same, and if they were victorious, their victory could inspire other women to fight back too. And this could only happen now that her name and lawsuit were on the tongues of everyone in the industry.

Then she stopped in her tracks, her shadow already halfway across the street. Everyone knew she had been fired. Everyone knew she was suing Whilt. *We're not hiring that troublemaker.* The words echoed in her ears. That was why she hadn't been called in for interviews. A feeling of nausea rose up within, so strong she almost turned around, stroller and all, and dove into the bushes. No. She took a few deep breaths, exhaled, drew in a few more breaths, and then crossed the street to the safety of the other side.

Tears streamed down her cheeks. Her career in finance was over. Her career working for any company was probably over. She wasn't being alarmist. She understood the mindset of the industry. Sure, there might be a few companies with progressive attitudes and understanding managers, but from Wanda's experience, they were not in the majority. What was left for her to do?

Wanda wanted to turn back the clock and return to a normal life. She wanted to forget about teaming up with Kate, even though the idea had made her happy just minutes ago. She wanted to get her name out of those newspapers to save her career. But none of these wishes would come true.

Wanda blew her nose noisily, causing a sleeping Nelly to grimace, and wiped her eyes.

No, she told herself. *Stop.* It was time to grow up. She needed to forget about the damage done, the uncertain future. All of that was beyond her control. The only thing she could control was her case. She told herself to be grateful for the meeting with Kate, for the possibilities that lay ahead legally speaking. She shook her head as if to eliminate the fears and lugged the stroller down the steps into the subway.

Chapter 41

The latest report in one of the online tabloids suggested that Wanda Julienne and Kate Mancini, both involved in lawsuits against Whilt, were spotted entering the law firm of Lambert, Klauss, Gervais and Dupuis. *Sources say Julienne and Mancini are collaborating on their cases,* the report said. Wanda scanned the text as her heart raced. Reporters were following them? *Who cares about us and our cases?* she thought.

"More people than you think," Kate answered an hour later on the phone. "Everyone knows how Whilt treats female employees, but the company has yet to really pay for it. Secretly, everyone wants to see companies like this get caught."

The two women had spent the previous morning meeting with their attorneys. Kate had been authorized to take a taxi to the office as long as she could recline during the meeting. They had indeed decided to collaborate, with the two attorneys discussing technicalities, and Wanda and Kate answering questions. It was the first time Wanda had felt involved in the case since her initial meeting with Lambert.

Wanda hung up the phone and sank onto the couch, rubbing her eyes. But her phone didn't remain quiet.

A small, uncertain voice on the other end of the line introduced herself as Rachel Swift, an analyst in Whilt's London office. Wanda recognized the name and before the woman continued, she knew what was coming. Now that the case was attracting more attention, women who had similar experiences at Whilt had begun to reach out.

Rachel described her situation. She was pregnant with her first child, and Whilt had just taken two of her industries away.

"Pretty soon I'll be left with nothing to analyze, nothing to do!" she said.

"Why did you decide to call me?" Wanda asked.

"For advice… after I read those reports about your case and Kate's. I'm seven months along, and now I have to manage the fatigue of pregnancy with not knowing what's going to happen with my job." Wanda could hear the tears in her voice.

"You have time on your side," Wanda said, grasping for straws. She wasn't like Galina, who always came up with smart advice in a split second. "You have to focus on your pregnancy and delivery right now, Rachel."

"But I can't wait like a sitting duck," she mumbled.

Yes, exactly. She couldn't recommend that this woman wait, as she did, expecting the company to miraculously realize she was a star employee. That wouldn't happen.

"In the meantime, meet with an attorney, discuss the situation. Be one step ahead."

And Wanda gave the same advice to another woman who called her a day later.

The idea that several women faced the same situation at Whilt—at present or in the past—troubled Wanda. She felt helpless. But maybe by setting an example and answering a few questions she wasn't so helpless after all?

Maybe she was encouraging these women to stand up for their rights too. Maybe that wasn't so scary. Maybe it was a bit rewarding. And it was thanks to Galina, who realized that Wanda didn't have the right to make this an individual problem, a closely kept secret of her own.

Chapter 42

Apologies weren't easy for Wanda. Not because she had a gigantic ego, but because she didn't consider herself very eloquent. Wanda was all about numbers and analysis. She was emotional, certainly, but had trouble transforming those emotions into words. That was probably why she had procrastinated for days—no, weeks. Even as she had walked out on Galina, she understood her friend's point. But she couldn't bring herself to turn back and explain. It was easier transferring her anger about her impossible situation to her best friend.

By the time she stood in front of that familiar door, hand poised to knock, it was a warm Friday afternoon in early June. How many calls from Galina had she ignored? Dozens. Galina could have shown up on her doorstep, but she wouldn't. Not due to indifference. Galina had the incredible power of timing. She knew Wanda wasn't ready, so she would wait. Even her phone messages weren't insistent. She would say "Hope you're doing OK" or "I called to see how you've been" or "Give me a call or stop by whenever you'd like."

And the moment had arrived.

Galina kissed her on both cheeks and squeezed her hands.

"I've missed you and Nelly," she said.

"I've missed you too." Tears welled up in Wanda's eyes, and she suddenly felt like a child who had been pouting for too long in her bedroom.

"It's OK." Galina put an arm around her and led her inside.

"But I haven't apologized yet."

"You don't have to," Galina said with a half-smile.

Then she unfastened the stroller straps and cradled Nelly in her arms. "How you've grown!"

Wanda wanted to throw her arms around her friend. Galina didn't need to hear a soliloquy or a formal apology. She just *knew*. Wanda hated herself for putting this distance between herself and the person who knew her so well and who cared about her so much.

"Don't," Galina said, as if reading her mind. "Everything's all right."

They settled onto the couch, and Galina prepared the usual—tea, accompanied by a box of butter cookies. Anya skipped into the room and threw herself at Wanda, who inhaled the sweet apricot scent of her soft, curly hair.

"Auntie Wanda, come play with me and Natasha in the nursery," she begged, pulling Wanda by the hand. Wanda happily let herself be guided until Galina intervened.

"Anya, how about this? Nelly will come and play with you and the nanny. Wanda and I have to catch up."

Her voice was kind but firm, and her solution readily accepted. Even with children, Galina had amazing bargaining powers.

After they handed Nelly over to Natasha and as the sound of Anya's laughter rippled through the hallway, they returned to the couch facing the Eiffel Tower. Wanda turned away. It was still difficult to look back in that direction, across the tower to her former life.

Instead, she kicked off her sandals, curled up in the corner of the couch and held her cup to her nose. She'd always found the scent of Earl Grey soothing.

"You have a nanny now?" she asked.

"In part for Anya's Russian. Natasha's worked wonders in a matter of a month. My Russian is shamefully rusty. I figured a nanny was the best solution."

Wanda nodded and took a sip of tea. The flowery taste was just as soothing to the palate as the odor was to the nose. It was a reminder of the afternoons she and Galina had spent this way, lounging on the couch and chatting about any subject under the sun. On some occasions, they spoke of nothing important; on other occasions, the conversations could be life-changing. This would be one of the life-changing days.

Wanda took a deep breath. She wouldn't take the easy way out, even though Galina had given it to her.

"I'm sorry for walking out on you," she said. "I'm sorry for not realizing you were doing the best thing for me, and when it comes to legal issues, I should trust you rather than wonder why you didn't ask for my uneducated opinion." Wanda rolled her eyes at her own behavior.

Galina smiled and shook her head.

"No, you were right about something—something important."

"What's that?" Wanda's voice was guarded. She didn't want her friend to humor her as if she was a child who couldn't accept her own bad behavior. She would handle the situation as an adult.

"I always seem to know better when it comes to you, yet I never allow you the same latitude when you observe my behavior." Her dark eyes weren't wistful. Instead, as was typical with Galina, her expression was decisive and firm. She had noticed something amiss, and she would rectify it. Wanda remained frozen, all except for her heart, which raced a mile a minute. An important declaration would follow. She could feel it.

"You were right," Galina continued. "These past months—these past few years, really—I've been living vicariously through Charles, through his cases or the cases of other friends still at the firm. I never let go. I told myself that part of my reason for taking a sabbatical was noble: I was doing the best thing for Anya. But I wasn't. I can only do the best for my daughter if I'm at my best. And I'm not at my best if I avoid a difficult situation instead of facing it. I was a coward."

"You're going back?" Wanda asked.

"Not entirely." Galina took a sip of her tea, but her eyes never left Wanda. "I've decided to move to the other side, the employee side. I'm tired of defending employers. I'm looking into starting my own practice, so I can balance the roles of mother and attorney as I see fit. And if you would like—if the offer still stands—I would be honored to play a role in your case."

Wanda set her cup on the coffee table and threw her arms around her friend. Galina laughed.

"I'm glad you have such faith in me, Wanda. But I'm not going to do things much differently from your attorney. I don't plan on taking this case away from him. That would be a mistake. Even though I understand Lambert passed the case on to another attorney at the firm, they've started the process and have done quite a bit of research. I propose joining the team, and doing it pro bono."

Wanda didn't have to answer with a longwinded discourse. The expression on her face sealed the deal.

Chapter 43

Wanda studied the name and phone number: Michael Smith of *The Times*. She'd scribbled it down even though she swore to herself she wouldn't call him. She would not make herself and her case a public spectacle. But since the day he had called her out of the blue, Wanda realized this wasn't about gaining a spot in the limelight or trying to make a name for herself in a sleazy, dishonest way. Whether she spoke with the press or not, the outcome of her case would be the same. Especially at this point. She no longer needed witnesses to come forward. By speaking to the press, she would be helping other women in the same situation. At Whilt and at other companies.

Her collaboration with Kate and reconciliation with Galina had put her in a generous frame of mind. She no longer felt alone and on the defensive. She felt ready to step out of the shadows and show other women they could do the same.

Wanda left Nelly at Galina's place with the nanny and then headed to the café where she had agreed to meet Michael Smith, the newspaper's Paris correspondent. She dashed through the rain, her ballerina flats filling with water with each splash.

Michael told her he would be wearing a blue scarf and sitting at the back of the café. He recommended his usual place on the Rue des Martyrs. Wanda made her way past the wooden tables to the dim corner where a young man sat, pen in one hand, coffee in another.

"Michael Smith?" she asked, even though he could be none other.

"That's me." He must have been in his twenties, hardly out of internship territory. He had eager brown eyes and a firm handshake. "Thanks for agreeing to the interview."

Wanda grimaced as she dropped her bag at her feet and settled into the rickety chair that one would never find at a café in her old neighborhood. "The word 'interview' makes it sound intimidating. My life never attracted this sort of interest before, so I'm not used to the attention."

Michael laughed. "That's the case with most people before they make the news. You've got to start somewhere. But don't worry, it'll be painless."

Wanda ordered a coffee, then took a deep breath as she watched Michael glancing at his list of questions. At least he wasn't intimidating. He was an ordinary young journalist, not one used to interviewing celebrities or big name politicians. This somehow comforted her.

They made small talk until Wanda's coffee arrived, hot and fragrant—a soothing distraction. She dunked the small gingerbread cookie and bit into the sweet softness.

"Tell me how everything started, Wanda—can I call you Wanda?"

She nodded. "No need to be formal."

And then she began her story. She didn't accuse Whilt of anything, only presented the important elements from start to finish. Michael jotted everything furiously in his notebook, stopping her only a few times to ask a question.

Normally, Wanda hated talking about the Whilt situation. With Max and Galina, she'd worried about their reactions, what they would expect of her. With her attorney, she had been concerned about having all the right answers so he could build a case. With her parents, she dreaded the aftermath: being badgered on a weekly basis about finding a job or a wealthy husband. Only as she told the story to Kate had she begun to speak with authority rather than shame. And that was the dominant characteristic as she told her story in the back of the unpretentious neighborhood café.

This confidence meant the story didn't come across as the whining of a dissatisfied employee. Instead, Wanda brought forth real, significant points as well as legal and sociological issues that applied to many other women, many other cases.

"Interesting," Michael repeated over and over, shaking his head and writing simultaneously.

And he didn't know the half of it. After all, Wanda had only talked about the parts relating directly to her job, performance, firing and contract. She wanted to keep the story serious and on track since she wasn't doing this to fuel the rumor mill. She was doing this to denounce the sort of practices that had ruined her career and were ruining the careers of other women—and that's what she told Michael.

"You think your career is ruined?" he asked. "Why?"

"Whilt's practices aren't unique to Whilt. You read about this sort of thing—the glass ceiling, discrimination—present at many companies in many fields. I just so happen to work in finance, but it's not a problem unique to finance. When I apply for a job elsewhere, those managers see I've stood up for justice, to the point of taking my employer to court. Who wants to hire someone who has the nerve to sue?"

Michael finished noting Wanda's words, then set down his pen and looked at her curiously. "Off the record, what are you going to do now?"

"I don't know."

"You look pretty serene for someone facing that kind of uncertainty."

"I wasn't always. I wasn't until just recently. When I realized I didn't have a choice so I might as well accept things as they are."

"Well, thanks for agreeing to this interview. I think it's going to be a good story."

"At least now you have the truth. I was getting tired of reading the rumors and suppositions."

Michael smiled. "Yeah, my editor will be thrilled with this."

Wanda glanced around at the calmness of their surroundings. A few regulars sitting with newspapers, chatting with the waiter or bartender.

"Is your office in this neighborhood, or do you live around here?" she asked

"I live here and work from home. No budget for an office in Paris."

"Looks like it could be a fun place to settle down. I used to think the sixteenth was the only livable spot in Paris, but maybe I was wrong."

"You in the market for a new place?"

"I just moved a few months ago, to a neighborhood I can't connect with. It was in a rush, so I didn't have much of a choice. It's been difficult. I can't move now, but it's nice to have a look around. To be ready next time."

"I highly recommend this neighborhood—and most of Montmartre really."

"I know someone who lives in Montmartre," she murmured, thinking once again of Max.

Chapter 44

When Wanda pictured Galina handling her case, she imagined playing a day-to-day role, being more involved in the details than she'd been with Lambert. But in reality, Galina's involvement meant more of the same.

Constance Dupuis, a partner at the firm and one with extensive experience in discrimination cases, was the perfect attorney for this case, Galina had said as she and Wanda met with the woman for the first time.

Wanda couldn't help but admire the woman's pristine white Chanel suit against the ebony of her perfectly straightened hair. She must have been in her mid-fifties, but she looked ten years younger.

Looks, however, were secondary to Ms. Dupuis' knowledge and sharp analytical skills. She and Galina quickly found themselves on the same page as they discussed the elements in their possession, the strengths and weaknesses of the case, and the plan of action. Wanda listened, entranced, but her presence in the room with these great legal minds would be restricted to this initial meeting.

"Why?" Wanda asked as she and Galina sat at a small

bistro over plates of roasted chicken and summer greens.

Galina pushed her sunglasses to the top of her head and leaned closer. The tables were empty around them as many Parisians had already headed off for their famous summer vacations, but Wanda and Galina were used to lowering their voices to share secrets.

"It's time for you to start living your life, to move forward. Your lawsuit is my job and Constance's. You've provided all the essential information, and if we need anything further, we'll ask. But you are not an attorney, Wanda, so you have no business hanging around the office and discussing strategy with us."

Wanda chewed on a forkful of chicken and sighed. Galina was right, but it was hard to let go of what had become her life over the past nine months. Nine months. Like a pregnancy. That was the problem; she had treated this whole situation as a new part of her life, a new baby. But it wasn't. It was something she had to set aside, to be handled by professionals. She had to move on, to find her place.

Her phone rang, and Max's name flashed across the screen, as if some sort of sign. Galina glanced at the phone before Wanda had time to send the call directly to voicemail.

"You are being a fool, letting him get away." Galina sipped on her mojito and stared at Wanda with the expression that always broke her down.

"Galina, you don't understand." Wanda sat back and pressed her fingers to her temples. "It's not that I don't care about him. I just need to get past this case and find myself in a better position. My only choice now is to depend on Max, and I don't want to do that."

"He won't wait forever. He'll go on with his own life. You even said he was dating. That's an accident waiting to happen. Do you realize how many women would snap him up in about ten seconds? I know you're worth waiting for, Wanda, but do you want to take the risk? Think about it."

Chapter 45

The Times article filled Wanda's heart with pride. Her words sounded eloquent and professional, honest and sincere. And as she read the story over and over, she realized the importance of her message. She emailed Michael a thank you, for truthfully telling her story, for making her voice heard. And he quickly replied, thanking her for sharing her story and asking her to keep in touch with further developments.

The next development, however, was one Wanda wouldn't share with the press and one Wanda hoped her attorneys could manage to prove false in the courtroom.

It was a hot afternoon, too hot to remain in a top floor apartment without air conditioning. So Wanda had taken her laptop, along with Nelly in her stroller, to the park. It was easy to find a quiet spot, alone on a bench near a cluster of rose bushes, on an afternoon like this, when most other people were at work.

Wanda was thankful for the massive plane trees that provided her and Nelly amnesty as the sun beat down and any sort of breeze remained scarce. She scrolled through the job listings, her usual occupation, and with one hand rolled the stroller back and forth to lull Nelly to sleep. Just as she dozed off, Wanda's phone vibrated. Galina. She answered it in a half whisper.

"Nelly must be falling asleep," Galina said.

"You know our routine well."

"Do you have a minute to talk?"

"Yes." Wanda's heartbeat accelerated. Her friend's tone was enough to signal something was wrong. "What is it?"

"How well do you know Flora Fortin?"

"Well, I... We used to go out for drinks with some of the others. But that was before maternity leave. We talked a lot less since I got back. She never really understood how my priorities changed. Why?"

"She's provided an affidavit, basically saying that the two of you worked closely together and she had been present during your conversations with Louis—and that nothing inappropriate took place."

"What?" Wanda shrieked and stood up, sending her computer sliding onto the seat. She paced in front of the bench, her breath caught in her throat in such a way as to block any words from forming.

"It's OK, calm down. We know this is a lie. This happens quite frequently in these sorts of cases, Wanda. Flora was probably put in a situation where it was either her or you. She chose to save her ass, as most people in her position would have done."

"So what do we do? This means it's my word and Kate's against her and Louis... and God knows what other Whilt employee they'll force into testifying!"

Wanda lowered herself to the bench. She was shaking like a leaf, in spite of the hot temperature and blazing sun.

"Your testimony and Kate's are important. But I would be lying if I said we didn't need other witnesses."

Wanda's mind raced. She thought of Maddie, who

had offered to testify. But now, in light of Flora's statement, her confidence disintegrated. Could she trust any current or former Whilt employee? What if Maddie betrayed her at the last minute? A couple of years ago, Wanda would have never believed Flora would do such a thing.

"Let me think about this, Galina," she said.

"All right, you have a few days."

"But the trial isn't until—"

"Wanda, we need time to prepare this case. We don't want to scramble at the last minute. I don't work that way."

Wanda leaned against the hard wooden bench, turned off her computer, turned off her phone. She gazed at Nelly sleeping peacefully and tried to focus her mind on productive thoughts. She would consider Maddie. She would reconstruct each of their conversations, as if somehow, she would find a clue previously overlooked. Could she take the risk of calling this woman to testify on her behalf? She didn't know the answer. As much as she pondered and analyzed, she didn't know who she could trust.

Chapter 46

Wanda and Galina sat in the twin black leather chairs in Constance Dupuis' office. Galina with her legal pad and favorite fountain pen, and Wanda with one hand clutching the other in her lap. Ms. Dupuis glanced from one to the other from behind a stack of papers pertaining to the case.

"I don't know what to suggest," Wanda said with a sigh.

"You'd said you had an idea," Galina said, impatience in her voice.

"A woman named Maddie Rosenberg recently left Whilt and signed a nondisclosure non-disparagement agreement. She told me that if she were subpoenaed, she would be willing to support me."

"But you don't trust her?" Galina asked.

"I don't know who to trust any more. That's the problem." Wanda played with the ends of her hair, giving her nervous hands something to do.

"What are your reasons for trusting her, and what are your reasons for doubting her?" Ms. Dupuis asked.

Wanda thought for a moment, then replied, "She's

always been honest with me in the past and has gone out of her way to warn me about the problems I would face at Whilt. That's why I would trust her. As for doubting her… I would doubt anyone who signed an agreement of any sort with Whilt. I haven't seen the agreement. I don't know what it contains. And if some people—like Flora—dare to lie under oath for Whilt, I imagine others could do the same."

Both attorneys were silent, their eyes on Wanda.

"What would you do?" she asked, glancing from one to the other. "Who would you trust?"

Ms. Dupuis spoke first. "Galina and I will discuss the matter. There isn't an obvious answer. But we depend on your guidance since you know Ms. Rosenberg."

"Do you have one feeling that outweighs the other, Wanda?" Galina asked. "Based on your personal experiences with Maddie."

Wanda closed her eyes and let her mind wander, scrolling through images, words and memories.

"It's too much of a risk," she said, her eyes flying open. "We'll make do without her."

"You have doubts then?" Ms. Dupuis asked. She doodled on the corner of a legal pad even as her eyes found Wanda's.

Wanda nodded. "I guess I do." Then she turned to Galina. "Based on feeling, she wouldn't betray me. But I can't trust my feelings, Galina. I have to eliminate all risks. And Maddie's testimony is a risk. What would happen if she backed up Flora? I would lose everything, wouldn't I?"

"It's not as clear cut as that," Galina said, sighing. "But of course it would be extremely negative."

"I refuse to take that risk."

In Wanda's mind, the matter was settled.

෨֊ᕽ

Wanda brought takeout sushi to Kate's apartment, and Kate hugged her with delight.

"How did you know I've been craving sushi?"

Kate led her down the hall to the sitting room and lay down in her usual spot. Her powder blue maternity dress unfolded around her like a fan.

"I'm so tired of this couch," she grumbled. "Only another month."

They chatted about this and that, and then Wanda brought Nelly into the nursery to play with Kate's daughters. Nelly tugged at Wanda's jeans for a minute or two, then crawled off toward a rather tempting stack of board books as the girls chased after her.

"Luckily your girls like playing with little ones," Wanda said as she returned to the sitting room and sank into the plush cushions.

"Have a California roll," Kate urged, pushing the box in Wanda's direction. "They're lovely."

Wanda took one but had trouble concentrating on the food. She was too busy thinking about her case.

"How do you manage?" she asked. "With the baby arriving any time and giving nearly full control to the attorney working on your case."

"You have to learn to let things go, Wanda. That's what I've done. To a certain degree, we have to be involved, to provide information, to help each other out as we've done. Then it's the lawyers' turn to take over. I've stopped thinking about the case. My doctor put his foot down during my last appointment. I don't have a choice if I hope to have a healthy delivery."

Wanda could have told Kate about Flora's false testimony but decided against it. She didn't want to add stress to her friend's shoulders, especially as her due date approached.

Before she left, she promised Kate she would follow her lead, leaving the case to the attorneys and turning her focus back to where it should be—to her daily life.

Chapter 47

Wanda studied her reflection in the bathroom mirror. Her cheeks looked a bit rounder, the dark circles under her eyes had lessened. She managed to wash her hair regularly. She was beginning to look more like Wanda Julienne with each passing day. Her meeting with Kate and her interview with *The Times* reporter had marked a turning point. Her case was anything but resolved, but she now realized that she had made some courageous decisions over the past several months, and her actions might help others in similar situations. That made her proud.

But sadness remained in her eyes. She couldn't hide it with extra layers of mascara or oversized sunglasses. And even if she could hide the sadness from others, she couldn't hide it from herself. She felt it in her heart when she looked at Nelly and saw the smile that should have made her smile. Instead, that smile reminded her of Max. He continued to send her checks, and they piled up on the counter. She preferred a steady diet of pasta and potatoes, interrupted only by better meals at Galina's table, to falling into a routine of dependence.

Wanda planned to continue down this road of stubborn dissidence, to carry on with a deepening sadness in her heart. She had grown used to this routine of ignoring her own desires and her own happiness.

A knock at the door interrupted her thoughts. She was expecting Galina, who had told her to get dressed, put on some makeup and sit tight. Galina hadn't explained the reason for her impending visit, but Wanda figured it was related to her case. *Strange it would be in this part of town though,* she thought.

Galina marched into the apartment, threw her summer white handbag to the floor and asked Wanda to join her on the couch.

"What's this about? Everything OK with the case?" Just as Wanda was about to enter panic mode, Galina put a hand on her arm and spoke.

"This isn't about the case. It's about Max."

"What about him?"

"I ran into Rich this morning. Max is about to sign on for another medical mission."

Wanda felt as if her heart had dropped into her stomach.

"He's not going to wait around forever, Wanda."

"But he just got the job at the hospital. I thought—"

"He signed a nine-month renewable contract at the hospital. It ends in September."

"So he's not renewing." Her voice was dull, empty, a reflection of her heart.

"Well, wouldn't you do the same if the person you loved kept slamming the door in your face? Would you want to remain in the same city?"

"Maybe not." Wanda stood up and paced, hands to her face. All of a sudden, she accepted the feelings she hadn't wanted to accept. All of a sudden, she understood that she couldn't avoid risk entirely. All of a sudden, she acknowledged that she should have followed her heart.

"It's too late," she hissed. "I've made a mistake, and it's too late."

"No it isn't, silly," Galina said. She stood before Wanda and forced her to look into her eyes. "I didn't come here to drop bad news in your lap and then take off. I'm all about action, and you know it. Rich told me nothing is official yet. Max has another week to decide. And I happen to know he's off work today. I suggest you hightail it over to his apartment and take control of your future."

"But what about Nelly? I—"

"What do you think I'm here for?" Galina pushed a few bills into Wanda's hand. "I've called a taxi. It's waiting for you."

Chapter 48

Wanda's heart pounded as the taxi driver sped through town and up the hilly streets of Montmartre. He swerved around a corner and parked in front of the building Wanda hadn't been to for months. She climbed the rickety wooden staircase that slanted in certain spots and smoothed out when least expected. Then she stood at Max's door.

What would she say? The short taxi ride hadn't given her enough time to plan. But she knew that even a two-day taxi ride wouldn't have given her enough time. The door opened before she had a chance to knock. Max stepped back, and she nearly jumped.

"I guess we're both surprised," he said. He was dressed in jeans and a T-shirt and looked a bit disheveled as he often did on his days off.

"You were going out. I can come back if it's not a good time." Wanda's words stumbled over each other, and she looked down in discomfort.

"No, it wasn't anything urgent." He took a step back. "C'mon in. Excuse the mess, though. I've been working a lot lately so not much time for house cleaning."

"As if I'm the greatest housekeeper?" she said, following him to the couch. He pushed aside a pile of newspapers, and she sat at the edge of a cushion, hands folded in her lap. She was a nervous wreck, and that was impossible to hide.

"So I'm guessing you're here for a reason," he said. He had given up on coaxing her into a relationship. It was clear by the distance in his eyes and the nonchalance of his words.

"I'm sorry," she said before she could lose the courage to pronounce the words. Her eyes remained focused on the embroidered edge of her beige skirt, the light color a contrast to her even paler skin. "I pushed you away, and I shouldn't have. I refused to believe in you, and I refused to believe in myself. For me, everything—everyone—represented a potential for betrayal. I didn't think you could love me enough to want to go through all of this with me."

Then she looked up, into eyes that showed a hint of the emotion of the past.

"If it's too late, I understand. But if it isn't too late, I wanted to say… I love you."

And then, before he could reply, Wanda stood up and rushed out the door.

"Wanda!" He called out her name and hurried down the steps, but Wanda had become an expert at running away. She made it to the pavement in record time and lost herself in the sinewy streets of Montmartre.

⊱⊰

"He wasn't home," she told Galina when she returned to her apartment an hour later.

"Damn!" Galina shook her head. "Maybe he was out on an errand. Go back. I can stay with Nelly."

"No, I can handle this, all right? I'll call him."

Galina sighed, looking into Wanda's eyes as if she could read them. *She probably can*, Wanda thought. *She probably knows you're lying.* But Wanda couldn't explain to Galina her reason for running. She couldn't even explain it to herself. She'd cried the entire way home, then hastily wiped her eyes at her front door and told her friend she had cried out of disappointment.

"I'll stay here with you," Galina said.

"No, I'm fine." Wanda's words came out with more firmness than she'd intended. Galina knitted her eyebrows as she gathered up her handbag.

"I'm sorry. I didn't mean to sound so snappy. I'm just exhausted."

"That's OK, Wanda." Galina took her by the hands and looked at her with sympathetic eyes. "Get some rest—please. And don't forget to call him."

"I won't," Wanda promised.

Wanda went about her daily routine as if nothing had happened, as if she hadn't proclaimed her love to Max and then run out the door. She didn't allow herself to cry, didn't allow herself to regret the words that seemed so awkward as she played them over and over in her mind. She glanced at her phone, hoping for a call or message from Max even though she would never admit it. And then it was bedtime, and she cried herself to sleep.

Chapter 49

Three days passed. Wanda avoided offering Galina information about the Max situation. "I left him a message, and I haven't heard back." Galina had seemed puzzled but didn't press for further details. And her friend didn't have time to get too involved now that the workweek had begun. Galina had thrown herself into Wanda's case with gusto—as Wanda had expected—so had little time for unrelated conversations.

Friday evening rolled around, and Wanda treated herself to a bath. The one good thing about the ramshackle apartment was it had a decent bathtub. She filled the tub with lavender bath salts and settled in for a soak. Nelly had finished her bottle in record time and slipped into a peaceful sleep.

Wanda tried to block out thoughts of the case and thoughts of Max, the two subjects troubling her. She attempted a meditation technique until the water became so cold that she decided bath time was over. She wrapped herself in her terrycloth robe, unwound her hair from its knot on the top of her head and sank onto the couch. A gentle knock at the door. Or maybe just a sound outside?

Wanda didn't move. The knocking—it was indeed knocking—was louder this time. She approached the door and glanced out the peephole. Max. She wouldn't get her hopes up. He was probably here to tell her of his decision: that he would be leaving in September.

With trepidation, she opened the door.

"Hi," she whispered.

"Nelly sleeping?"

"Yeah."

She took a step back, and he followed her inside. He'd worked today—she could tell by the fatigue in his eyes—but he'd stopped home to shower—she could tell by the soapy scent.

Wanda turned to face him as they stood beside the couch as if not knowing whether to sit or stand. She crossed her arms and tried to look unbothered, indifferent even.

"Look, I understand if what I said was too late. No hard feelings, OK?" She would rather stem the bleeding than face total humiliation. Better to save a bit of her pride.

But Max just shook his head, took her hands and drew her closer. His eyes carried that expression, that sparkle, they had months ago, and Wanda's heart skipped a beat.

"Wanda, I love you," he said. "I tried to tell you the other day—"

"Why didn't you—"

"Come by earlier? I almost did. But I had something to take care of. You see, I wasn't sure if I wanted to stay here without you. I was ready to sign up for another medical trip, but for the wrong reason. I was looking for an escape. I wanted to escape the pain of life without you and Nelly. It was wrong, I know. These missions are extremely important and deserve doctors who commit for the right reasons."

Wanda's mind was racing. He wasn't going. He had chosen her. She let herself take a step closer, and closer, until she was in his arms, her heart pounding against his.

Chapter 50

Approaching the broad nineteenth century building, Wanda walked between Galina and Constance as if they were her bodyguards. The attorneys wore their traditional black robes, creating a picture of austerity. There was much ceremony and history in a French courtroom. Wanda refused to look left or right, only straight ahead at the massive ancient structure, flanked by naked plane trees.

They climbed to the top floor, and Wanda gazed out the wall of windows to the street below. Passersby carrying shopping bags or briefcases went about the daily routine; for most people, today was like any other.

In the hallway, Wanda spotted three Whilt human resources employees, the company's attorneys and Louis. She shuddered at the sight of them. Physically, they had been out of her life for months, yet their presence remained, a grim shadow following her every move. They looked the same as always and chatted pleasantly amongst themselves. When they tossed a glance in her direction, she nodded politely, then turned away.

In her corner, she had her attorneys and Max for

moral support. Her heart should have been beating a mile a minute, but she felt strangely calm and confident. The panic and worries of the past months had reached a maximum only to collapse as she had collapsed into Max's arms. And from that point until the trial, a sense of stability had taken over.

Before they entered the courtroom, Galina pulled her aside.

"Whilt's attorneys will say some unpleasant things about you, they will say things we know aren't true." Galina's voice was firm, but her eyes were kind. "No matter what they say, you are to remain quiet. Constance and I are handling this case—not you. You are only to speak if an attorney or judge asks you to speak. Is that understood?"

Wanda had prepared herself for the worst; she was ready for any insult, any lie. She nodded and shot one last glance at Max, who would remain in the back of the room. His eyes communicated a multitude of messages that filled her with strength.

The courtroom, with its antique wood and scalloped designs on high ceilings, normally would have captured Wanda's eye, but she hardly noticed a thing as she slid onto the bench next to her attorneys. Her eyes were on the judge, the lawyers, Louis, and her own hands fidgeting in her lap.

Wanda remained passive as both sides presented their points. She cringed as the Whilt attorney spoke of her "abysmal fund performance," without mentioning that Thomas had been the one to sink her funds while she was away. And she clenched her jaw when the Whilt attorney suggested that any sexual harassment was a figment of Wanda's overactive imagination. Galina glanced at her, but Wanda wouldn't even catch her eye. She kept her gaze down at her knees, where her fingers twisted her black silk skirt into knots.

It was only when Constance called a witness to the stand that Wanda's eyes rose to meet those of her best friend.

The risk had frightened Wanda, but it hadn't frightened Galina. Maddie would take the stand.

Epilogue

One Year Later

"Have a good evening," Wanda called out over her shoulder to Kate as she dashed down the hall. It was their first week in business together. Kate had put up the cash to start a fund management operation, catering to women and families. It was the two of them so far, but they had already received applications from analysts and fund managers—some Whilt employees on the edge as Wanda and Kate had both been such a short time ago.

They shared office space with Galina, in a sixteenth arrondissement building around the corner from Wanda's old apartment. From the windows, the top of the Eiffel Tower peeked through the trees. But Wanda hadn't returned to the old neighborhood full time; she hadn't sought another apartment where she could look out the window and wave to her best friend.

She and Galina were closer than ever, yet Wanda no longer had to cling to her as a psychological crutch. Their friendship was no longer off-balance, with Galina as the strong leader and Wanda as the weak follower. They were now on the same level, sharing successes and failures. And it felt good.

"I have to thank you," Galina had said to her one day as they unpacked boxes in the new office space.

"For what?" Wanda asked, wiping sweat from her brow. "Getting you into this moving mess?"

"No, for daring to stand up to me, for spurring me to wake up and take charge of my life."

"I can thank you for the same thing," Wanda said. "Except you didn't have to 'dare' as it's not that difficult to stand up to me."

Galina laughed. "We're even then?"

"Even."

Wanda thought back to the conversation as she rushed down the stairs and into the street, the chill of fall making her shiver in her unbuttoned trench coat. She was about to head back to the apartment she and Max had recently rented on the Rue des Martyrs, the street she had discovered during her interview with *The Times* reporter. She loved their eighteenth century building, and their apartment in particular, with its small balcony overlooking the busy street below. It was a nice change, doing business in one neighborhood and then going home to another, far from thoughts of the office. Because once she was home, she didn't think of work any more. She thought of Max, Nelly and the positive pregnancy test she'd taken that morning. She set a hand on her stomach and smiled. She would have news for Max when he returned from the hospital tonight.

Wanda buttoned her coat, looked toward the subway station, and then walked in the opposite direction, accompanying the wind and crackling leaves along the wide sidewalk.

Wanda rarely thought of Whilt and the experience that had torn apart her life for more than a year. Even though Galina had been an integral part of it, she never sparked memories of those dark days. Sometimes Wanda would remember how Galina had taken the bet Wanda had feared—asking Maddie to testify—and how that bet had led them to an easy victory. She could still see the look of shock on the Whilt attorney's face.

Wanda never told the press—and her attorneys never told the courtroom—about everything that had gone on at Whilt. She hadn't spoken of Raymond Grant snatching her hotel room, Jim Tuxford singing *Singing in the Rain* in the middle of the office, or Tricia Warren sleeping her way to the top. She didn't talk about Xavier exposing the bitcoin scandal and losing his job, Elodie throwing herself out a window or Maddie negotiating her way out of a difficult situation.

Those events illustrated the dysfunctional nature of Whilt, but Wanda and her attorneys didn't need them to prove that management had mistreated her. She had plenty of concrete evidence, so why go with the outrageous occurrences that people outside of Whilt might not believe?

Wanda stopped in front of the familiar glass tower and looked up at the windows that had held her captive for so many years. She hadn't been back here since she had shut down her computer for the last time.

If you haven't experienced the lunacy, it's easy to view it as that: lunacy, delirious visions in a confused mind, Wanda whispered to herself. *But if you've spent any time at the Creepshow, and you're not drinking too much of their Kool-Aid, you'll know it's true.* Then she turned around and walked away, her silhouette blending with the others against the Parisian sky.

Travel to France again in *Paris, Rue des Martyrs,* another novel in the *From Paris to Provence* series!

A Note from Adria Cimino

Dear Reader,

Thank you for reading *Paris Jungle*. I wanted to write a novel that would reflect what a lot of women have experienced in the corporate world. The more people talk openly about workplace discrimination and harassment, the better we can fight it!

If you enjoyed *Paris Jungle*, I'd love it if you left a review on Amazon.com. Reviews help other readers discover books. Even a few sentences saying why you enjoyed it can make a big difference. Thank you, your words count!

I would also like to invite you to sign up for my newsletter to stay up to date on my new releases and special sales: https://bit.ly/cimino-news. I only send a few newsletters per year, and I'll send you my short story *Flore* when you sign up!

If you want to journey back to France through the pages of a book, you might like another one of my novels, *Paris, Rue des Martyrs*. It's about four strangers in Paris whose lives entwine in meaningful ways.

All the best,
Adria

P.S. Read on for a sneak peek at *Paris, Rue des Martyrs*.

Discover more by

BEST-SELLING AUTHOR
ADRIA J. CIMINO

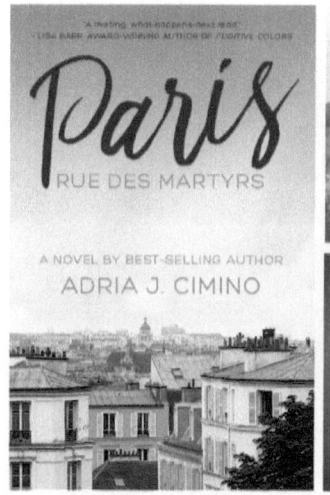

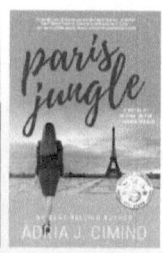

Find out about new releases and deals
by signing up for Adria's newsletter:
https://bit.ly/cimino-news

(She'll even send you *Flore* for free!)

Paris

RUE DES MARTYRS

A NOVEL BY BEST-SELLING AUTHOR
ADRIA J. CIMINO

Chapter 1

Rafael

Rafael Mendez arrived like a thief in the night at 120 Rue des Martyrs. He ran all the way from the train station, where he had left one small, ragtag suitcase in a rented locker. His sneakers slapped noisily along the cobblestones, then pavement, in time with his own tears and the rain falling from a grim Parisian sky.

It was as if each minute lost counted for everything in his 23-year-old life. He pushed past umbrellas that seemed to tango as they bobbed against one another, old men who chatted with no one in particular, couples laughing, and a few sidewalk café tables left behind to weather the storm.

He was nearly blind to this first vision of the city, and only looked up now and again at the street signs to reassure himself that—yes—he hadn't lost the Rue des Martyrs. And then he stopped. He pushed wet strands of long, black hair back from his face, wiped away the silly tears of that odd combination of desperation and excitement, and sank down onto a bench facing the address he had imagined all of his life in Colombia.

Now, as the rain soaked through his jeans and his gaze traveled across the street to the only lighted apartment in building 120, his mind returned home. That's where his quest began, after all. In Bogotá.

❦

As a child, he would play with the emeralds. That was his first memory. Not mother. Not father. Emeralds. Because that was how his life began. His father never wanted to tell Rafael that the French jewelry designer gave birth to him on a trip for those precious stones. He only said it once—grimly—shaking his head and staring at the dark sand under their feet. Rafael remembered looking up at him with widened 10-year-old eyes as they plodded along the dusty trail to where his father would buy the stones. It was Rafael's first trip there with his father, and in the young boy's mind, it became a sacred place.

But he couldn't think of that story right now or those fucking emeralds. It was over. He had to erase every memory from his mind, the images that haunted him at night.

The one remaining light in 120 snapped off, leaving the building in darkness. It would be too late. He was wasting time. His heart raced as he crossed the street between the cars that kicked up muddy water onto his jeans. He ignored the honking horns. He wanted to move forward, and all at once he wanted to travel back. Rafael was frightened. Afraid of what he might learn or might not learn. Never be afraid, his father had hissed into his ear on that first trip for emeralds.

Before he could let his worries swallow him up with one great gulp, he pounded his fist on the heavy, brown-lacquered door that like a clamshell closed the apartments to the world. Nothing. The sound of his fist against the wood reverberated through his entire body, but no one responded. He scolded himself for his own impatience. How could he possibly have expected someone to answer that door at 11 o'clock on a Thursday night? He placed his hand softly against the handle and sighed, knowing he should leave, yet not able to abandon the glimmer of hope that his problems would be resolved in a matter of hours.

The door creaked open suddenly, and he jumped back.

"There's no need to be startled, you know. When you knock on a door like a maniac, you should expect it to open."

A wispy redhead slipped through the doorway and onto the sidewalk. She gave him a crooked grin, lit a cigarette and leaned against the cool brick.

"So," she said, blowing smoke to the sky, "who do you want to see that badly?"

Something about the young woman struck him. She wasn't beautiful, with her almost pasty complexion and skinny figure in oversized jeans, but she had an assertive air about her that was much more impressive.

"It must be pretty serious," she continued, taking a drag. "Why don't we talk about it?"

"Do you know a woman named Carmen?" Rafael asked, his voice shaking.

"No."

"Someone named Carmen lives or lived here…" he said, his words trailing off. He felt ridiculous and unprepared as he faced such inquisitive eyes.

"A lot of people have been around here," she said. "I need specifics."

"That's the problem. I don't have any."

"What have you come here for anyway?"

"Answers."

She flicked her half-smoked cigarette into the gutter and with green eyes paler than any emerald gazed up to the sky.

"What are your questions?"

A window flew open from above and a woman's voice called out: "Laurel? Laurel…"

The person who had to be Laurel pulled Rafael against her and ducked into the shadows. She grinned mischievously.

"I've got to run."

His heart skipped a beat as her hair brushed against his cheek. But he kept any flicker of sentiment in check. He didn't have time for distractions.

"Meet me back here tomorrow—same hour," Laurel whispered. "I'll see what I can find out. I have some connections…" And then she slipped away from him and into the night.

Find out what happens next… Pick up *Paris, Rue des Martyrs* now!

About the Author

Adria J. Cimino is an author of contemporary literary fiction and a partner in the boutique publishing house Velvet Morning Press. She lives in Paris with her husband, daughter and son. When she isn't writing, you can find Adria at her neighborhood café watching the world go by.

Keep up with Adria online:

Newsletter: https://bit.ly/cimino-news
Website: AdriaJCimino.com
Facebook: AdriaJ.inParis
Twitter: @Adria_in_Paris

Acknowledgements

I would like to thank those who supported me and never turned their backs when times were tough—you know who you are. And thank you to all of the important women in my life who know that when we stand together, we are strong.

Finally, as always, thanks to the talented and hard-working team at Velvet Morning Press, and to my writing group the Paris Authors Group!